Muriel Barbery is the author of four previous novels, including the IMPAC-shortlisted multimillion-copy bestseller *The Elegance of the Hedgehog*. She has lived in Kyōto, Amsterdam and Paris and now lives in the French countryside.

Alison Anderson is an author and the translator of around 100 books from French, including Muriel Barbery's previous novels and works by Amélie Nothomb and J. M. G. Le Clézio.

Praise for *The Life of Elves*:

'An enigmatic and beguiling fairy tale . . . Barbery explores the mystical connections between nature, art and the human heart with vividness and clarity' *New York Times*
'This is a truly enchanting story, beautifully told and rich in meaning . . . this book truly deserves to be read by story lovers of all ages' *Irish Times*
'This fervent, idiosyncratic fable is undeniable evidence of a richly lyrical imagination.' *Kirkus Reviews*
'Vivid imagery and a thread of mystery draw readers into the timeless and ethereal world' *Booklist*
'An emotional, entertaining examination of magic in the modern world' *France Today*

Praise for *A Strange Country*:

'The novel could be read as an allegory for the challenges that face our modern world, from the controversy surrounding our borders to climate change. Or, it may be seen as a strange and poetic fantasy similar to the work of Tolkien. In either case, it is a beautiful book about what it means to be brave and how we all must work to save ourselves and each other' *San Francisco Book Review*
'Bewitching . . . [an] enchanting hero's journey' *Foreword Reviews*
'A mix of J. R. R. Tolkien and Hayao Miyazaki, epic in scope yet grounded by humor' *Publishers Weekly*
'Readers who love meditative, dreamlike fiction will enjoy this translation, which rings with the music of the original French' *Booklist*
'A marvellous mixture of fairytale, poetry, fable and adventure story' *Le Figaro*

Also by Muriel Barbery

The Elegance of the Hedgehog
The Gourmet
The Life of Elves
A Strange Country

A Single Rose

Muriel Barbery

A Single Rose

Muriel Barbery

Translated from the French
by Alison Anderson

Gallic Books
London

A Gallic Book

First published in France as *Une Rose Seule*
by Actes Sud

Copyright © 2020 by Actes Sud
English translation copyright © Europa Editions 2021

First published in Great Britain in 2021 by
Gallic Books, 12 Eccleston Street, London, SW1W 9LT

This book is copyright under the Berne Convention
No reproduction without permission

All rights reserved
A CIP record for this book is available from
the British Library

ISBN 9781913547110

Typeset in Fournier MT by Gallic Books
Printed in the UK by CPI (CR0 4YY)

2 4 6 8 10 9 7 5 3 1

to Chevalier, always
to my dead

on the roof of hell

1

It is said that in ancient China, during the Northern Song Dynasty, there was a prince who, every year, would have a field of a thousand peonies planted, and during the first days of summer their petals would ripple in the breeze. For six days he would sit on the floor of the wooden pavilion where he habitually went to admire the moon, drinking a cup of clear tea from time to time, and he would observe the flowers he called his girls. At dawn and at sunset, he would pace up and down the field.

Early on the seventh day he ordered the massacre.

His servants would lay out the lovely, murdered victims, their stems severed, heads pointing to the east, until only a single flower was left standing in the field, its petals offered to the first monsoon rains. And for the five days that followed, the prince stayed there, drinking dark wine. His entire life was contained in those twelve revolutions of the sun; all year long, he thought of nothing else; once they were behind him, he took a vow to die. But the hours he devoted to selecting the chosen one, then delighting in their silent tête-à-tête, held so many lives in one that the months of mourning were not a sacrifice to him.

What he felt as he gazed at the survivor? A sadness shaped like a sparkling gemstone, shot through with flashes of such pure, intense happiness that his heart faltered.

A Field of a Thousand Peonies

W hen Rose woke and, looking around her, did not understand where she was, she saw a red peony with sullen petals. She had a vague sense of regret or lost happiness. Ordinarily, this inner agitation scratches at the heart before vanishing like a dream, but on occasion time is transformed, and gives the mind new clarity. That is what Rose was feeling that morning in her encounter with the peony, which revealed its gilded stamens to her from its exquisite vase. For a moment it seemed to her that she could stay for ever in that bare room, gazing at that flower, feeling *alive* as never before. She studied the tatami mats, the paper panels, the window opening onto branches in the sun, the crumpled peony; finally, she observed herself, as if she were a stranger she had only met the previous day.

The evening returned to her in waves – the airport, the long drive through the night, the arrival, the lantern-lit garden, the woman in a kimono kneeling on the raised floor. To the left of the sliding door through which she had entered, branches of summer magnolia spilled from a dark vase and caught the light in successive cascades. The shadows on the walls shimmered like gleaming water pouring onto the flowers, and all around there was a strange, quivering darkness. Rose could make out walls with sand finishes, flat stones that led to the raised flooring, secret spirits – an entire twilit life suffused with sighs.

The Japanese woman had led her to her room. In the next room, steam from a bath rose from a large basin made of smooth wood. Rose had slid into the scalding water, captivated by the bare simplicity of this damp, silent crypt, its wood decor, its pure lines. Stepping out of the bath, she wrapped herself in a light cotton kimono, the way one might enter a sanctuary. In the same way, she slipped between the sheets with an inexplicable feeling of fervour. Then everything faded away.

Now there came a discreet knock, and the door slid open with a soft hiss. The woman from the night before set a tray down by the window, her steps short and precise. She said a few words, took gentle, sliding paces backwards, then knelt down, bowed, and closed the door again. As she disappeared from view, Rose saw her lowered eyelids quiver, and was struck by the beauty of her brown kimono and its obi belt embroidered with pink peonies. The memory of her clear voice, each sentence ending on a clipped note, chimed in the air like a gong.

Rose inspected the unfamiliar food, the teapot, the bowl of rice; every movement she made felt like a desecration. Through the bare frame of the window, whose glass pane and paper screen slid open, she could see the etched, trembling leaves of a maple tree and a more expansive vista beyond. There was a river, its banks teeming with wild grasses, and on either side of its pebbled bed were sandy pathways and more maples mingling with cherry trees. Midstream, in the languid current, stood a grey heron. Fine-weather clouds drifted overhead. Rose was struck by the force of the flowing water. Where am I? she wondered, and although she knew this city was Kyōto, the answer stole away from her like a shadow.

There was another knock. Yes? she called, and the door opened. The peony sash reappeared; this time, the kneeling woman said:

Rose-san get ready? and pointed to the bathroom door. Rose nodded. What the hell am I doing here? she thought, and although she knew she had come for the reading of her father's will, the answer still eluded her. In the vast empty chapel of the bathroom, next to the mirror, a white peony with petals lightly dipped in carmine ink was drying like a new painting. The morning light pouring through an opening latticed with bamboo cast fireflies onto the walls and, for a moment, immersed in the kaleidoscopic play of a stained-glass window, she could have been in a cathedral. She got dressed, went out into the corridor, turned to the right, retraced her steps after reaching a closed door, then followed the meanders of floor and paper. She turned a corner, and the partitions became dark wood with sliding panels, and round the next corner, she found herself in a large room with a live maple tree in the centre. Its roots burrowed deep into folds of velvety moss; a fern caressed the trunk, next to a stone lantern; all of it was surrounded by glass panelling, open to the sky. In the shards of a fragmented world, Rose saw the wood floor, the low seats, the lacquered tables, and, to her right, in a large clay vase, an arrangement of branches with unfamiliar leaves, vibrant and light as fairies, but the maple tree punctured the space in which Rose's senses were drowning, and she felt the tree drawing her towards it, her breath responding to its magnetic force, as if it sought to make her body into a shrub with murmuring boughs. After a moment she escaped from the spell, went over to the other side of the inner garden, where large windows looked out onto the river, and opened a panel that slid soundlessly along its wooden rails. Along the banks with their cherry trees ran morning joggers, and Rose would have liked to slip into their steps that had no past or future, no ties or history; would have liked to be nothing but a moving point in the flow of seasons and mountains passing over cities on its way to the ocean. She looked beyond the river. Her father's house was built at a certain height, above a sandy path visible through the tree branches. On the opposite bank were the same cherry trees, the same sandy pathway, the same maples and, further still, overlooking the river, a street, more houses – the city. Finally, on the horizon, a tumble of green hills.

She returned to the sanctuary of the tree. The Japanese woman was waiting for her.

'My name Sayoko,' she said to her.

Rose nodded.

'Rose-san go for a stroll?' asked Sayoko.

Then, in accented French, blushing slightly: '*Promenade?*'

Again those clipped sentence endings, like an echo, those pearly, shell-like eyelids.

Rose hesitated.

'The driver outside,' said Sayoko. 'Wait for you.'

'Oh,' said Rose, 'all right.'

She felt rushed, and behind Sayoko the tree called to her again, strange, seductive.

'I forgot something,' she said, and dashed away.

In the bathroom, she found herself facing the white peony, with its blood-lacquered petals and its snowy corolla. Hyoten, she murmured. She stood there for a moment, then, picking up her canvas hat, she left the chapel of silence and water and went out to the hall. In the daylight, the magnolia blossoms were curved like butterflies – how do they do that, she wondered irritably. Outside the house, the driver from the night before, in a black suit and a white cap, bowed when she appeared. He held the door open for her respectfully, closed it again gently. In the rear-view mirror she studied his eyes, thin lines of black ink blinking without revealing their iris, and, oddly, she liked the abyss of that gaze. Before long, he gave her a childlike smile that lit up his waxen face.

They crossed a bridge and, once they were on the other side of the river, headed towards the hills. She got her first glimpse of the city in a tangle of concrete, electric wires, and neon signs; here and there, the outline of a temple seemed to be adrift on the tide of ugliness. The hills drew nearer, the neighbourhood became residential, and finally they drove the length of a canal lined with cherry trees. They got out of the car below a street crowded with shops and wandering tourists. At the top, they went through a wooden gate – Silver Pavilion, said the driver. His lack of presence surprised her, as if he had absented himself in order to focus solely on her and whatever she needed. She gave him a smile, and he responded with a little nod.

And so they entered an ancient world of wooden buildings with grey tiled roofs. Before them stood strange tall pines set in squares of moss; stone walkways meandered past beds of fine grey sand where parallel lines had been drawn with a rake; a few azaleas had been invited. They went through the gate that led to the main gardens. On the right, next to a pond, with the help of its graceful roofs the old pavilion seemed to be taking flight, and Rose had the unsettling impression that it was breathing, that organic life had taken refuge in these ageless partitions and galleries, these white paper openings, casting their long, milky reflections onto the water. Straight ahead stood a tall mound of sand with a levelled summit; to the left a vast expanse of the same sand stretched out, striped with parallel grooves and curving at the far end into waves on a shore. The overall view revealed first the mineral flow, then the imitation mountain with its flattened summit and the pavilion with its winged roofs; further away, the ponds with their quicksilver water, pine trees pruned like birds preparing for flight, a few more azaleas; everywhere, age-old stones were surrounded by flat, luminous moss and rooted in the embankments. Finally, the gardens wound their way to an esplanade where the crowd of visitors had massed. Between Rose and the esplanade, maple trees rustled in a cascade of lacy foliage, descending in tiers down the side of the hill.

She was overwhelmed by the beauty, the stone and wood, by both the torpor and intensity; I can't go through this again, she thought, with a mixture of tiredness and terror. But then immediately afterwards: there is something here. Her heart began to pound, she looked around for somewhere to sit. *Like in the land of childhood.* She leaned against the wooden gallery in the main building; an azalea caught her eye; the terror and joy infusing the mauve petals merged into a new emotion, and she thought she was at the heart of a sanctuary of pure, icy water.

They followed the visitors' path and paused for a moment on the little wooden bridge that spanned the grey water on the way to the maple trees and the upper levels of the garden. All around the ponds there were other strange, tall pine trees. Rose looked up and took in the branching of the needles against the sky; the dark tree trunks were projecting the earth's force in these flashes of plant lightning; she felt herself being sucked into a flow of clouds and moss. The driver's steps were measured; he turned around from time to time to wait for her, showing no impatience, setting off again when she gestured to him. His tranquil pace had a calming effect on Rose, restored to the world a touch of reality which the power of the garden dissolved in the trees. Now the path lined with tall green bamboo led to a stone stairway; she could have reached out to either side to touch the velvety moss where the maples spread their roots. With each step she took, the branches created a tableau of perfection, and the visual choreography of it touched her heart but also irritated her – and yet her irritation, she realised with surprise, was doing her good. At last they came out onto the little esplanade; below them were the pavilion, the wooden buildings, the grey tiled roofs, the sculpted sand; beyond lay Kyōto and, further still, other hills. We are East, said the driver and, pointing to the horizon: West mountains.

She assessed the city. Everything about it was related to the presence of the mountains that, to the east, north, and west, enclosed it at right angles. In reality they were high hills, their shapes giving the impression of height. Green and blue in the morning light, they flowed towards the city with their gentle tree-covered slopes. Ahead of her, beyond a small hill, the city seemed ugly, full of concrete. Rose's gaze returned to the gardens below, and she was struck by their *precision* – the unyielding, obvious fact of them, their purity sharpened with sorrow, the way they were able to revive childhood sensations. As in dreams she used to have, she was struggling in dark, icy water, but in broad daylight, in a profusion of trees, in the blood-specked petals of a white peony. She leaned her elbows on the bamboo railing, stared at the neighbouring hill, looked for *something* there. The woman next to her smiled.

'Are you French?' she asked, in an English accent.

Rose turned to her, saw her wrinkled face, grey hair, well-cut jacket.

Not waiting for an answer, the woman continued.

'Wonderful, isn't it?'

Rose nodded.

'The result of centuries of devotion and abnegation.'

The Englishwoman laughed at her own words.

'So much pain for a single garden,' she said, with a light, frivolous tone.

But she was looking intensely at Rose.

'Well,' she said, as Rose still hadn't spoken, 'perhaps you prefer English gardens.'

She laughed again, idly stroking the railing.

'No,' said Rose, 'but this place is overwhelming.'

She felt like talking about the icy water, hesitated, decided not to.

'I just got here last night,' she said in the end.

'Is this your first trip to Kyōto?'

'It's my first trip to Japan.'

'Japan is a country where people suffer a great deal, but they don't seem to mind,' said the Englishwoman. 'In return for this indifference to misfortune, they harvest these gardens where the gods come for tea.'

Rose found this irritating.

'I don't think so,' she said. 'Nothing can make up for suffering.'

'Oh, really?' asked the Englishwoman.

'Life is painful,' said Rose. 'You can't expect any good to come from that.'

The Englishwoman looked away, lost in contemplation of the pavilion.

'If a person is not ready to suffer,' she said, 'they are not ready to live.'

She stepped back from the railing and gave Rose a smile.

'Enjoy your stay,' she said.

Rose turned to the driver. He was watching the Englishwoman as she vanished below the maple branches, with a look of both hostility and fear. Rose started down the hill. When she reached the last of the black stone steps that led to the pond in front of the pavilion she stopped, overcome by the thought that no one, anywhere, was waiting for her. She had come to hear the reading of her father's will, a father she had not known; her entire life consisted of this succession of ghosts who told her where to go and gave her nothing in return; she was always headed towards emptiness and icy water. She recalled an afternoon in her grandmother's garden – the whiteness of the lilacs, the short grass at the edge of the estate. The Englishwoman's words came back to her and, with them, a surge of rebelliousness. Never again, she said out loud. She gazed at the grey water, the pavilion, the sculpted sand, the maple trees, the garden's large expanse of childhood and eternity, and she was engulfed by a tide of sadness mingled with flashes of pure happiness.

2

In ancient Japan, in the province of Ise, on the shores of a cove concealed from the ocean, there lived a healer. She knew the properties of plants and used them for those who came to her begging for relief from their afflictions. In spite of this, she herself – as if the gods had made an irreversible, inalterable decision – suffered constantly from the most terrible pain. One day, a prince she had cured thanks to one of her carnation teas said to her: Why don't you use your powers to heal yourself? Because my powers would disappear, she replied, and then how would I heal my fellow man? What care you for the suffering of others if you could live without enduring such pain? asked the prince. She laughed, went out to her garden, cut an armful of blood-red carnations, and handed them to the prince, saying: To whom, then, would I, with a light heart, give my flowers?

An Armful of Blood-Red Carnations

At the age of forty, Rose had not really lived. As a child she had grown up surrounded by magnificent countryside, where she became acquainted with fields and clearings, ephemeral lilacs, blackberries, and bulrushes; and then, in the evening, under cascades of golden clouds and washes of pink, she began to understand the world. As night fell, she read novels, and in this way, through pathways and stories, her soul was crafted. Until one day, as if losing a handkerchief, she lost her predisposition for happiness.

She had had a gloomy youth. To her the lives of others seemed sparkling and graceful, while her own life, when she tried to think about it, slipped away from her like water through her fingers. Although she had friends, she did not feel drawn to them; lovers drifted through the scenery like shadows, she spent her days in the company of indistinct figures. She had not known her father – her mother had left him just before her birth – and all she had known of her mother was melancholy and absence. So Rose had been stunned, upon her mother's death, to feel such terrible sorrow. Five years had passed, and she referred to herself as an orphan, although she knew that there was a Japanese man somewhere who was her father. She knew his name, knew he was rich. Her mother had occasionally spoken about him, indifferently; her grandmother said nothing. From time to time, she supposed he must think about her; at other times, since she was a redhead with green eyes, she became convinced that Japan was something her mother had made up, that her father didn't exist, that she had been born out of nowhere – she did not form any attachments, no one was attached to her, the void was eating away at her life in the same way it had created her.

And yet, had Rose been able to see herself as others saw her, she would have been astonished. They saw her deep hurt as conferring mystery, her suffering sounded like modesty, people thought she led an intense secret life, and as she was pretty, yet austere, she was intimidating and kept any desire at a distance. The fact that she was a botanist, on top of everything, only increased people's caution; botany was an enigmatic field, and she came across as elegant, a rarity, so in her presence they didn't dare talk about themselves. With the men who passed through her life, she made love so nonchalantly that she gave nothing of her feelings away. What was more, she never felt desire for more than a few days, and she preferred cats to human beings. She valued flowers and plants but was kept from them by an invisible veil that obscured their beauty and deprived them of life – and yet she felt that something, in that bark and those familiar corollas, was quivering and trying to befriend her. But the years were passing, and the icy water of her nightmares, a black water in which she was slowly drowning, gradually came to dominate her days. Then her grandmother died; she had no more lovers, no longer saw friends; icebound, her life was shrinking. One morning a week earlier, a lawyer had informed her that her father had died, and she had boarded a flight for Japan. She never questioned her departure; in the void that was her life, it mattered as little as all the rest. But her glum compliance with the lawyer's request masked a thirst that Kyōto was now revealing.

Following the driver, she passed once again through the main gate of the sanctuary and down the street with the little shops. Rose-san hungry? he enquired. She nodded. Simple food, please, she said. He seemed surprised, thought for a moment, then set off again. Beyond the canal they turned left, down towards the street below, until they reached a little house with a sign outside on the pavement. Ducking under a short curtain, the driver entered through a sliding door, and she followed him into the single room with its smell of grilled fish. In the middle of the room there was a huge extractor hood above a charcoal grill; to the left, a counter with eight places; to the right, behind the oven, shelves sagging with dishes and various utensils above a small worktop; on a low sideboard, bottles of sake stood against sand-coated partitions decorated with drawings of cats. All told, the decor of wood and chaos somehow reminded her of the cheap restaurants of her childhood.

They sat down at the counter, and the chef appeared, a big man wrapped in a short kimono over matching trousers. A waitress brought them hot towels. Rose-san eat fish or meat? asked the driver. Fish, she replied. He ordered in Japanese. Beer? he then enquired. She nodded. They fell silent. Around them vibrated a presence that their silence revealed, a suggestion of innocence pervaded the untidiness of the place, and Rose felt the world pulsing to some ancient rhythm – yes, ancient, she thought, even if that has no meaning. And again: we are not alone here. The waitress set down before them a lacquered tray of little containers filled with unfamiliar food, as well as a small dish of sashimi, a bowl with rice, another with clear soup. She said something apologetically. Fish coming soon, the driver translated. The chef put onto the grill two fish that looked like mackerel, speared with wooden skewers. He was sweating profusely and kept wiping his face with a white towel, but Rose did not feel disgusted the way she would have in Paris. She took a sip of ice-cold beer and bit into a piece of white sashimi. Ink fish, said the driver. She chewed slowly. The silky mollusc caressed her palate as images of cats, lakes, and ashes filled her mind. Without knowing why, she felt like laughing until, a moment later, a sharp blade fell – but on what? – and from something that should have been painful, a keen pleasure was born. She took another sip of beer, tasted a piece of red sashimi (fat tuna, he said) that set her senses reeling; so much pleasure born of such bare simplicity, she thought with wonder, as the waitress brought the grilled fish. With her chopsticks, she struggled to pull the flesh apart, concentrated, eventually opted for a slow, painstaking strategy, and met with success. The taste of the fish was subtle, but she wasn't hungry any more; she felt unusually calm.

They went back to the house. A man was waiting for her there, a Westerner. He greeted her politely when she came into the room with the maple tree. Next to him Sayoko, her hands folded over her peonies, stood watching her. Rose remained silent. The man stepped towards her. She noticed that he moved in a particular way, crossed the now-liquid space as if navigating between two oceans of reality. She also noticed his light eyes, blue or green, and the line creasing his forehead.

'My name is Paul,' he said. 'I was your father's assistant.'

As she said nothing, he added: 'Maybe you didn't know he was an art dealer?'

She shook her head.

'Of contemporary art.'

She looked around her.

'I don't see anything contemporary here,' she said.

He smiled.

'There are many kinds of contemporary art.'

'Are you French?'

'Belgian. But I've been living here for twenty years.'

She guessed he must be roughly her age and wondered what had brought him to Japan at the age of twenty.

'I studied Japanese at university in Brussels,' he said. 'When I came to Kyōto, I met Haru, and I started working for him.'

'Were you friends?' she asked.

He hesitated.

'He was my mentor, but in the end, yes, you might say we were friends.'

Sayoko said something to him, and, nodding, he motioned to Rose to sit down at the low table to the left of the maple tree. She took her seat, feeling as if the life inside her was escaping, like air from a punctured balloon. Sayoko brought some tea in ceramic cups with the textured surface of ploughed earth. Rose turned hers in her hands, rubbing the irregularities.

'Keisuke Shibata,' said Paul.

She looked at him, not understanding.

'The potter. Haru has represented him for over forty years. He's also a poet, a painter, and a calligrapher.'

He took a sip of tea.

'How tired are you?' he asked. 'I'd like to go over the plans for the next few days with you; you must tell me how you feel.'

'How I feel?' she said. 'I don't think tiredness is a major factor.'

He looked her in the eyes. She was disconcerted, waited.

'No,' he said, 'but I'd like to know all the same. We'll have plenty of time to talk about the other factors.'

'Who says I feel like talking?' she asked, in an aggressive tone she instantly regretted.

He didn't reply.

'What is there to do?' she asked.

'We need to talk, and then see the lawyer on Friday.'

He was still looking her straight in the eye, expressing himself in a calm, unhurried way. Sayoko reappeared at a door on the other side of the maple, came in to pour some more tea, and then stood there, looking questioningly at Paul, her hands on her pink peonies.

'There's a peony in the bathroom,' said Rose. 'It's called

Hyoten. It's grown on the island of Daikonshima, in volcanic soil. Does *hyoten* mean anything in Japanese?'

'It means icy water or, more precisely, the temperature of icy water, the freezing point,' he replied.

Sayoko looked at Rose.

'Volcano ice lady,' she said.

'You're a botanist,' said Paul.

So? thought Rose, feeling the same irritation she'd felt when she saw the magnolia blossoms at the entrance.

'He talked about you all the time,' he added. 'Not one day went by that he didn't think of you.'

The shock of his words came like a slap. He has no right, she thought. She wanted to say something, but only managed to nod, not knowing if she was agreeing, or refusing, or if she even understood what he'd said. He stood up: automatically she did the same.

'I'll let you get some rest, but I'll be back later,' he said. 'We'll have dinner in town.'

In her room, she collapsed onto the tatami, her arms folded over her chest. Delicately inserted into a black vase, their heads gracefully tilted, were three cavorting blood-red carnations. They were of the Chinese variety, with simple petals and fragile stems, their carmine colour exceptionally intense. The three corollas, the candour of the simple flowers, their perfumed freshness, all of it seemed a reproach to her; something about the way they were arranged unsettled her; a wave of exasperation went through her. She fell asleep. Two quick knocks on the door woke her with a start.

'Yes?' she said.

'Paul-san waiting for you,' came Sayoko's voice.

There was a moment of uncertainty, then she remembered.

'Coming,' she said, and thought: Bells, summons, chaperoned outings – this is worse than school.

She wondered how long she had been asleep. A long time, she thought. I'm jet-lagged, I always feel like I'm in the wrong time zone. In the bathroom mirror she saw that the pillow had left deep grooves across her cheek. On impulse she reached for a tube of lipstick, then put it back down. *He talked about you all the time.* She hurled the tube of lipstick as far as it would go, walked back through the bedroom, looked at the carnations, and calmed down.

She found Paul in the maple room.

'Shall we go?' he asked, coming towards her.

For the first time, she noticed he had a slight limp, and felt this explained the way he glided through the world like a fish in a river, creating fluidity from something broken. She followed him out to the hall, where the magnolia flowers vied to outperform each other in silent *entrechats*. They walked through the little garden that looked onto the street. The azaleas unfurled a firework display of pink and purple petals. At the foot of the stone lanterns, hostas burst from the same flat, velvety moss that was visible everywhere; on their right was a row of maple trees, on their left, a white wall where, in the early twilight, the shadows of a bamboo grove flickered.

'Where are we going?' she asked.

'Haru couldn't go out in Kyōto without being recognised. Kitsune was his secret refuge.'

As he had that morning, the driver took them to the other side of the river, and again they went through the streets of concrete and electric wires. Outside the restaurant, to the right of the sliding door, a red lantern looked to Rose like a lighthouse in the dark. Inside, the smoke blurred her vision. At the back, behind a counter crowded with sake bottles, the smell of grilled meat rose up into the air; at the front were four dark wood tables, the half-light brightened by a few hanging lamps; on the black painted walls there were manga posters, advertising signs, figurines of superheroes; everywhere there were crates of beer, enigmatic bottles, illustrated books; altogether the atmosphere was unusual, woody, and mischievous. Do all their restaurants look like the attics from our childhoods? she wondered, suddenly aware that she was hungry.

'I pictured Japan as a very sanitised sort of place,' she said, 'not somewhere you would smell the cooking oil.'

'We're not among Protestants,' he said, 'and I know what I'm talking about. Most of Japan is one happy chaos.'

'Not at his place,' she said, unable to say *my father's place.*

'Most of Japan,' he said again.

The chef stood before them, a young man in glasses and a headband, with protruding teeth. Rose noticed his timid curiosity as Paul exchanged a few friendly words with him; then she thought she heard her father's name, and the young man's expression changed. He took off his glasses and wiped them. There was a moment's silence, and then he said something, looking at her.

'Welcome,' Paul translated.

Was that all? she wondered.

'Do you eat meat?' Paul asked.

'What kind of restaurant is this?'

'Yakitori. Grilled meat skewers.'

'Sounds good,' she said.

'Beer or sake?'

'Both.'

There was a brief exchange between the two men, and after that she was alone with Paul in a wordless limbo that made her feel uncomfortable. She gave a start when the chef deposited two tall glasses of ice-cold beer in front of them. The same thought she'd had that morning – *we are not alone here* – crossed her mind again, and then, *What* is *this country where you're never alone?*

'Haru was from a modest background,' Paul said. 'This place reminded him of the yakitori he ate as a child in the mountains of Takayama.'

He raised his glass.

'Your health,' he said and, without waiting, took a long gulp.

Strangely, she thought of the three red carnations in their black vase. The chef brought a pile of meat skewers and a bottle of sake to the table. She drank down half her beer and felt better.

'The sake is from Takayama,' Paul said, pouring her a glass.

'Takayama? Are you trying to make things all sentimental?' she asked.

He looked her in the eye in that clear, direct manner of his that she found disconcerting and took a sip. She noticed the curve of his eyebrows, his high forehead marked with a vertical line. The sake was cool and fruity, soft on the palate; the meat was aromatic. She felt herself getting tipsy. She realised they had been eating in silence for a while already. Soon the meal would be finished, and they had hardly spoken. She relaxed, her initial embarrassment gone. When he began to speak again, she felt she was being roused from a peaceful reverie.

'Haru's greatest regret was that he was unable to give you anything during his lifetime.'

He can't do this, she thought, he cannot go on punching me in the stomach without warning.

'And why was that?' she asked, exasperated.

He looked at her, startled.

'I assume you know.'

I know, yes, I know, she thought angrily.

'Why did he regret it?' she asked again.

He took a sip of beer. His reply came slowly, as he chose his words carefully.

'Because he believed that it's through giving that one comes truly alive.'

'He was a Buddhist?' she asked. 'And you? Are you a starry-eyed believer, too?'

He laughed.

'I'm an atheist,' he replied. 'But Haru was a Buddhist, in his way.'

'In what way?'

'He was a Buddhist through his love of art. He believed Buddhism was the ultimate religion of art. But then he also thought it was the religion of sake.'

'Did he drink a lot?'

'Yes, but I never saw him drunk.'

He emptied his cup. She gave him a hostile look.

'I came here because I was asked to come.'

'I doubt that very much.'

She gave a bitterly ironic laugh.

'What can he give me now?' she asked. 'What can absence and death give me? Money? An apology? Lacquered tables?'

He didn't reply. They stopped talking, but as they left in the car waiting outside, as the night streamed down upon them like dark sap, as they went back through the garden with its lanterns and Paul said goodnight by the magnolia branches, she could feel, without knowing what it meant, the flowers at work inside her. She felt that something, in the bark and the corollas, was quivering and trying to befriend her. Exhausted, overwhelmed by the confusion of her thoughts, she fell asleep. During the night she had a dream in which she understood the arrangement of the carnations: they were asking to be taken, demanding to be an offering. She held out her hand, grasped the stems, pulled them out of the water, let them drip onto the tatami. Then, in the half-light of the same room where she was sleeping, she saw herself holding the three blood-red carnations out to Paul and saying, To whom, then, would I, with a light heart, give my flowers?

3

People say that the poet Kobayashi Issa, who, at the time of the European Enlightenment, was living a long, painful life in still-feudal Japan, went one day to Shisen-dō, a Zen Buddhist temple in Kyōto, where he sat for hours on the tatami admiring the garden. A little monk came to him to show off the fine nature of the sand, and the beauty of the stones, around which an absolutely perfect circle had been raked. Issa remained silent. The little monk eloquently praised the depth of the mineral scene before them; Issa still said nothing. The monk, rather surprised by his silence, extolled the perfection of the circle. And so, Issa, pointing beyond the sand and stones to the splendour of the tall azaleas, said: If you go beyond the circle, you encounter flowers.

You Encounter Azaleas

R ose awoke fully aware of the moon's presence. She saw it framed by the open window, pearly and solitary, and an image formed in her mind, a landscape of vineyards, and it seemed strange that it had come to haunt her here. It was hot, cicadas were chirring. She stayed there for a moment, eyes open, breathing slowly. The earth was turning, and she was motionless; the winds blew past her, and she stayed where she was. In this silence and darkness she was from nowhere, from no time. She fell asleep again.

On waking, she thought of the dinner the night before, the memory of it still vivid. She took a shower, got dressed, and went into the maple room, where she found Sayoko wearing a light-coloured kimono with an orange obi dotted with grey fireflies. As the Japanese woman gestured to her to sit down, and brought her the same tray as the day before, Rose again admired the translucence of her eyelids.

'Rose-san sleep well?' Sayoko asked.

Rose nodded.

'Driver say you meet *kami* yesterday,' she added.

'*Kami?*'

'*Kami*. Spirit.'

Rose looked at her, puzzled. *I met a spirit yesterday?* Then she remembered the Englishwoman at the Silver Pavilion and the expression on the driver's face as she walked away.

'The British woman?' she asked.

Sayoko looked cross.

'*Kami*,' she said again.

Then, with a crease of concern on her brow: 'Bad *kami*.'

She left the room, taking short, stubborn steps. Rose took pleasure in perfecting her technique for cutting fish with chopsticks – an unfamiliar fish, tender, buttery, which she chewed with a schoolgirl's satisfaction. She decided not to have any rice, poured a cup of green tea, breathed in the fragrance. A wave of emotion brought her to her feet, in need of air, and she went to open the window that looked out onto the river. The force of the water deterred her; she hurriedly returned to the room and found herself right up against the maple tree. Between earth and sky, rooted in its well of light, it absorbed the images conjured up by the cut-grass fragrance of the green tea – tears, wind over fields, sorrow. As the vision faded, she could hear her grandmother's voice in the distance, saying: Please, don't cry in front of the child. And then, as a door slid open somewhere in the house, Rose gave a start. Striding through the air in his fluid, uneven way, Paul was coming towards her, his arms laden with pink peonies.

'Ready for a tour?' he asked Rose, while Sayoko relieved him of the flowers.

Taken by surprise, she nodded. Outside, the driver was waiting. The weather was lovely, a bit cool, and she was surprised by how light she felt. Come on, she thought, it won't be for long, it never is. They went back over the river, but this time they drove up through the hills towards the north. They soon turned right up a steep hill and continued through a residential neighbourhood of grand houses. The driver stopped outside a wooden entrance.

'Shisen-dō,' Paul said. 'My favourite at this time of year.'

'Is it a temple?' she asked.

He nodded. They climbed a few steps and followed a paved walkway lined with tall bamboo whose grey stalks and yellowish thatch were like a roof of flint and straw. On either side of the path, a strip of light sand streaked with parallel lines was like a mineral stream, and Rose could feel the caress of its tranquil current, its delicate grain, its playful flaxen water. They went up some more steps and found themselves facing the temple. In front of the surrounding wall, a patch of the same sand was home to a single azalea bush. They removed their shoes and went in. Beyond a corridor, a gallery of tatami mats looked out onto the garden. Paul sat down in the middle of the open space, and Rose joined him. They were alone.

She saw nothing else. There were plants all around, a breeze through the trees, some rounded bushes, but all her life, its years and hours, were contained in the curved lines the rake had traced around a large stone, an azalea, and a clump of hostas, placed on sand so fine that it powdered one's gaze. The world was born out of this perfect ellipse; Rose's spirit was dancing with the sand, embracing the grooves, revolving around the stone and the leaves, starting over; there was nothing beyond this endless walk on the ring of days, on the loop of the senses; she felt as if she were going mad. She wanted to tear herself away, gave up, surrendered to the intoxication of the stone circuit. She looked further away and saw nothing. The world had taken refuge in this patch of sand and circle.

'We come here mainly in the spring to admire the azaleas,' Paul said.

A sudden intuition shot through her.

'Did he ask you to take me around like this? Did he come up with the itinerary? The Silver Pavilion, this temple?'

He didn't reply. She looked again at the ellipse, the sand, the lines of its inner worlds. Beyond, the large bushy azaleas formed a tender green rampart for the dry garden.

'I hadn't noticed the azaleas,' she said. 'I was looking at the circle.'

'In the Zen tradition, the circles are called *ensō*,' he said. 'They can be open or closed.'

She was astonished by the interest his words aroused in her.

'What do they mean?' she asked.

'Whatever you like,' he replied. 'Reality matters little here.'

'Is that why he wanted you to drag me around from place to place like an unwanted parcel, to dissolve reality in the circle, drown it in the sand?'

He said nothing, went on admiring the garden.

'You're a botanist, and you aren't looking at the flowers,' he said finally.

There was neither aggression nor judgement in his tone.

'My favourite poem is by Issa,' he continued.

He recited the poem in Japanese, then translated.

in this world
we walk on the roof of hell
gazing at flowers

She became aware of a recurring noise, which she'd first heard on their arrival at the temple, a sort of sharp clack regularly masking the music of flowing water. Suddenly something changed. The sand altered, shrank back, ran through into a familiar hourglass, faded away while the scene expanded, spread into the trees, the birdsong, the murmuring of the breeze. Now she could hear the current of the stream below them, the hollow bamboo swaying against the bed of stones with a sharp clack then going off in the other direction, continuing the flow of water. The maples, the Japanese iris and, everywhere, the azaleas rooted in the ancient sand – a quiver went through her until everything subsided and she was merely Rose lost in an unfamiliar garden. But somewhere, in a place where reality was of no importance, she planned to look at the flowers. They stood up.

'I suppose you'll be taking me to lunch in a place that he decided on,' she said.

'The restaurants weren't his idea,' he answered. 'But first I'd like to show you something.'

'You have nothing better to do than look after me?' she asked. 'Don't you have a family? Don't you work?'

'I have a daughter; she's in good hands,' he said. 'As for work, that will depend on you.'

She considered his response for a moment.

'How old is your daughter?'

'She's ten. Her name is Anna.'

She didn't dare ask about Anna's mother, was put out by the thought that she existed, then banished her from her mind.

Back at the house, in the hall, the morning's pink peonies cast a complex shape. She followed Paul; they went past her bedroom and right to the end of the corridor. He slid open the door where she'd had to turn back the day before. It was a room with tatami mats and two large picture windows at an angle, one overlooking the river, the other the mountains of the North. Facing east was a low table with a paper lamp, some calligraphy supplies, a few scattered sheets of paper; on the walls facing the windows were large panels of light-coloured wood. She looked first at the river, then the mountains with their peaks overlapping like folds of cloth, and finally she saw the photographs carefully pinned to the wooden panels.

On one of them was a little red-haired girl in a summer garden. In the background, tall white lilacs concealed a drystone wall. To the right, the eye was drawn to a valley of green and blue hills, a winding river, a sky of full-bellied clouds. She glanced at the other photos and, after a moment, realised that this was the only one that hadn't been taken on the sly. All the others had been shot through a telephoto lens without her knowledge, taken from various angles, in every season.

'How did he get this?' she asked, moving closer to the little red-haired girl.

'Through Paule,' he said.

'How?'

'One day, Haru received this photo from her.'

'That's it?'

'That's it.'

She gazed at the panels. The stolen prints showed her at every age with her grandmother Paule, with her friends, boyfriends, lovers. Rose knelt on the mat, lowered her head like a penitent. This sign that she was yielding, imploring, revived her anger, and she raised her chin.

'My mother's not in any of these photos,' she said.

'No.'

'He spied on me my whole life long. And not a single picture with her.'

'He wasn't spying on you,' said Paul.

She met his clear gaze, felt cornered, exasperated.

'What do you call all this?'

'It's all Maud left for him.'

'An entire life with no mother,' she said.

She stood up.

'And no father.'

She knelt down again.

'Did you have any idea he was watching over you?' asked Paul.

She didn't answer.

'You're angry,' he said.

'Wouldn't you be?' she murmured, pointing angrily at the photographs, mortified to hear the trembling in her voice.

There was yet another moment lost between two layers of perception. She looked at the little red-haired girl in the lilac garden; her anger continued to grow, and then, without warning, it was transformed. As a child she had experienced a rough draft of that full life we call happiness; the emptiness that came later had engulfed her very memory of it. Now that memory was brimming to the surface again, like a bowl overflowing with lovely fruit; she breathed in the fragrance of ripe peaches, she could hear the insects buzzing, she could feel time stretching languorously; a tune was playing somewhere, at the edge of what is called the heart, or the core, and she let herself drift upon it in a liquid world. Life was woven with threads of silver that wound through the wild grasses in the garden – she followed one of them, shinier, brighter than the others, and this time it kept on extending, continued endlessly into the distance.

'Anger doesn't come out of nowhere,' Paul said.

She roused herself from her wordless trance. In a silent crash, the curves of the circle re-formed, and she tried in vain to retain the lovely fruit, as if trying to hold on to a dream on waking up.

'According to Sayoko, the driver said I met a *kami* at the Silver Pavilion,' she said. 'A bad *kami*.'

He sat down next to her.

'I didn't meet anyone there. I just exchanged a few words with an Englishwoman, a tourist.'

'Sayoko and Kanto have a fairly personal vision of spirits,' he said. 'I'm not sure their classification is orthodox.'

'The Englishwoman told me that if you're not ready to suffer, you're not ready to live.'

He gave a short laugh, not aimed at her.

'Suffering serves no purpose,' she said. 'Absolutely none.'

'But it exists,' he said. 'What are we supposed to do about it?'

'Should we accept it just because it exists?'

'Accept it?' he echoed. 'I don't think so. But it's the same as freezing point. Just above freezing, an element is liquid. Just below, it's solid, a prisoner of itself.'

'What does that mean? That you have to suffer no matter what?'

'No, I just mean that once you go below freezing, everything congeals together – suffering, pleasure, hope, and despair.'

Hyoten, thought Rose. I've had enough of flowers.

'We are an obsessive family; my mother was all sadness, and I'm all anger,' she said.

'And your grandmother?' he asked.

On leaving the room, she glanced behind her. Framed by the picture window, the blue mountain ridges melted into a fine-weather mist that rose from the earth and erased their jaggedness and differences in height, varnishing the world with invisible ink, like a powerful, translucent ink wash painting.

In the car she felt like nothing so much as a bad-tempered child. The silence weighed on her, but she was loath to break it; she liked the restaurant Paul had chosen, but held back from complimenting him on it. They sat at the bar. Everything was smooth, light-coloured wood, unadorned, as bare as a hut. Across the room, in an alcove streaming with light, maple branches sprang from an earthenware vase as rough as an oyster shell. Paul ordered, and two beers arrived instantly. She thought they would eat in silence, but after a few sips he began to speak.

'Haru was born in the mountains near Takayama. The family home was by a torrent that was frozen for three months of the year. The family had a sake business in town; his father would come down the mountain every day on foot. Haru took me there, to stand before a huge stone in midstream, and he told me he'd grown up watching the snow falling or melting on that stone. The boulder had its vocation, along with the trees in the snow, the waterfalls, and the ice.'

Ice again, thought Rose.

'At the age of eighteen, he came to Kyōto with no money or training, but very quickly he became acquainted with everyone who had anything to do with making things, with *matter* – potters, sculptors, painters, and calligraphers. He made his fortune thanks to their work. He had a natural talent for business. And irresistible charm.'

He looked her in the eye. Once more she was annoyed, remembering resentfully the extraordinary magnolias in the hall.

'However, not a single day of his life was devoted to money. What he wanted was the freedom to honour, in his way, the stone of his native stream. And, from the moment you were born, to leave his daughter with a legacy that would give her solace.'

'Solace?'

'Solace.'

She took a sip of beer. Her hand was trembling. A chef appeared before them and bowed before reaching for some pieces of raw fish in a little refrigerated display case, to the left of the maple arrangement. She had not noticed that they were sitting next to a row of raw flesh, next to octopus tentacles and orange sea urchins; all she saw was the effort she had to make to stop herself being hurt by words and the dead, overcome with a weariness that was soon undone by the odd excitement this country of trees and stone intermittently aroused in her. The chef placed in front of each of them a square plate of grey and brown ceramic, as rough as a mountain path; on this earthen surface were marinated ginger and fatty tuna sushi, which she reached for as if it were a lifeline, in her desperation to have a body again, to escape her mind, to be nothing but appetite. The combination of tender fish and vinegary rice calmed her. With the relief that came from being in her body once again, she thought that she could understand her father, that she too would be saved by *matter*, by the clay of the world, by a bandage of flesh and rice. Nothing more was said during the meal. Paul took his leave of her by the pink peonies in the hall, saying, I'll come back this evening to take you to dinner; Kanto is at your disposal if you want to go into town this afternoon.

She lay on the tatami mats in her room. I'm walking on the roof of hell without looking at the flowers, she thought, and, at the same time, she saw again the luxuriant azaleas of Shisen-dō. As she was dozing off, she also saw a circle of extreme loveliness that formed again and again in her mind's eye, a circle of deep, lacquered ink floating between dream and reality, tracing an exquisite spiral. Then, as she became enchanted by its endless fluidity, the circle froze and at the same time opened up, creating a gap where a few clouds drifted.

4

In the Heian era, during the period when Kyōto was the capital of an archipelago lost in solitude, a little girl came one day at dawn to offer rice to the deities at the sanctuary of Fushimi Inari, an hour's walk from the city. As she was approaching the altar she saw, on one side, that during the night pale little irises had bloomed, spotted blue, with orange stamens and a deep purple heart.

A fox sat waiting for her, tucked among the flowers.

She looked at him for a moment, then handed him the rice, but he shook his head sadly until, feeling helpless, she picked an iris and held it up to his snout. He took the flower, chewed on it delicately, then spoke to her in a language she could understand – alas, the memory of his words has since been lost. What is known, however, is that the little girl went on to become the greatest lady of letters in classical Japan and that all her life she wrote about love.

She Picked an Iris

H alf asleep, Rose drifted for a moment, lulled by the rapture of the open circle, but before long the sensation vanished. Through the window, she saw the flowing river. She took her canvas hat and left the room.

In the large maple room there was no one. She ran her hand over the transparent window, and behind her she heard Sayoko's shuffling little steps. She turned: again, the rice-paper delicacy of those lowered eyelids. They stood for a moment facing each other in mute comprehension of the foliage; then the spell was broken, and Rose cleared her throat.

'I'm going out for a short stroll,' she said.

After a moment, she added: 'A *promenade*.'

She crossed the room, but at the last minute she turned and came back.

'Volcano ice lady?' she asked.

Sayoko stared at her and made a gesture that meant, Wait here. She left and came back holding a rectangle of white paper. Rose took it carefully, then turned it over.

'Daughter of father,' said Sayoko.

On the yellowed photograph was a boy roughly ten years old, half turned towards the lens; behind him a cascade of white water between snow-covered rocks; beyond, mountain pines, more icy stones, and dark undergrowth.

'Same look,' said Sayoko. 'Ice and fire.'

Rose resisted the urge to go down on her knees, lower her head, and let the world collapse upon the back of her neck. She studied the boy's eyes. The intensity of his gaze made the backdrop of snow and white water a well of darkness. She handed the picture back to Sayoko, turned on her heel, and fled. In the garden, she stopped. *I am like him.* She went through the bamboo gate, around the house, and onto the sandy path that followed the river. *I have red hair, and I am like him.* She walked for a while, drowning in the power of those dark eyes, the force of the torrent. The line that separates water from earth, the line between water and sky: floating lines, outlined a virgin territory with neither wind nor heat, neither ice nor birdsong, an enclave where matter dissolved in the void. A cyclist passed very close to her; she gave a start, realised she was clenching her fists, and came back to earth. The weather was fine, a large heron was lazing at the water's edge sheltered by rushes, walkers went by. Before long, the embankment grew wider, the sandy path became a strand, the wild grasses in the breeze took on the grace of feathers. Something was turning, slipping. She thought: How many people ever come to know their father through the child he once was? Surprised and troubled, indignant, too, she felt that this was a blessing.

Crowds of people were crossing a big bridge. She went up a stone ramp and joined the flow, borne westwards like a twig. The street led to a covered gallery lined with small shops, restaurants, and massage parlours. She had been walking for a long time, and was a long way from the house with no money or phone. She turned to the right and, a bit further on, entered a stationery shop that smelled of ink and incense; she went over to the blank scrolls hanging against a partition and figured out that they were used for the calligraphy traced on the delicate white square cards that were displayed below the scrolls, their corners held in place by fine cotton hooks. *Every day a new dream of ink*. Next to them, there was incense, too, and incense holders, brushes, fine paper, boxes with motifs of flowers and leaves; she would have liked this world to be her own, would have liked to dissolve in it in a blaze of fragrant wood, a dream of petals and clouds. As she was rubbing her finger lightly over a brush with a crimson handle, she felt someone near her, and she turned to find herself face to face with the Englishwoman from the Silver Pavilion.

'Kyōto is not such a big place; you always end up running into people,' said the woman.

Holding her hand out: 'I'm Beth. Are you enjoying your stay?'

She was wearing a white silk dress and, over her shoulders, a long, elegant jacket.

'Wonderfully,' answered Rose. 'I'm having loads of fun.'

'I can see that,' said Beth, although Rose could not decide whether she was being ironic.

'Do you live here?' Rose asked.

'More or less,' she replied. 'And you? What brings you to Japan?'

Rose hesitated and then, astonished, as if hurling herself off a cliff: 'I came for the reading of my father's will.'

There was a silence.

'Your father's Japanese?' asked Beth.

Rose nodded.

'You're Haru's daughter?' the Englishwoman asked.

Another silence. Am I Haru's daughter? wondered Rose. I am the daughter of a little boy from the cold mountains.

'You knew him?'

'Yes,' Beth said, 'I knew him very well.'

She glanced over Rose's shoulder.

'You're being followed,' she said.

Rose saw Kanto standing by the incense sticks.

'Here,' said Beth, handing her a business card. 'Call me when you have a moment.'

She gave an amused little wave in the direction of the driver and left the shop. Rose went over to Kanto.

'Shall we go back home?' she asked.

He seemed relieved, bowed, motioned to her to follow him. In the gallery, they turned right and before long were out in the open again, heading down a wide avenue, where he hailed a taxi. She was amused by the white lace on the seats, the driver's white gloves and theatrical cap. She felt mordant, bitey — *yes, bitey, if that means anything, I want to bite, I want to live to bite.* In the little garden outside the house, the purple azaleas were tastefully wilting, their petals crumpled along delightful creases, their branches set with dying stars. She went through the hall, brushing one of the peonies with her finger. In the maple room she found Paul sitting on the floor, his legs stretched out, ankles crossed, his back against the glass wall. He was reading. He looked up at her when she came in.

'I'm ready for the next rose-coloured roller coaster,' she said.

'Sarcasm suits you,' he replied.

Taken by surprise, she said nothing.

'You were a mischievous child,' he added, standing up. 'Anyone can see that from the photos.'

She hated what he had just said. To change the subject, she pointed at his book.

'What are you reading?' she asked.

'Poetry.'

The ideograms on the cover were like the fine tracings of a reed in the wind; in the gap in a perfect circle of ink, birds and clouds drifted.

'Who by?'

'Kobayashi Issa,' he replied.

'Ah, yes, of course, hell and flowers.'

'The roof of hell,' he said.

It seemed to Rose that they passed the yakitori restaurant from the night before and then, near the Silver Pavilion, turned into the street where she'd had lunch with the driver. The restaurant was indeed located almost directly opposite the childhood greasy spoon, and once again she found herself in a lost land, a reverie of wood, a dream of a life long gone. On the right, guests were welcomed to an elevated area with paper partitions, tatami mats, and low tables. On the left, a counter led to a work area with shelves above it sagging with magnificent tableware. Everything was brown, grey, ochre, and warm; calligraphy and scrolls hung from the sand-finished walls; there were tastefully crinkled paper lamps everywhere; she felt as if she could lose herself in this vanished way of life. They sat down at the bar. Above their heads, spilling from a hanging basket, fringed irises flickered like will-o'-the-wisps.

'Iris japonica,' she said, looking at the flowers, and then, 'What a lovely place.'

'Beer?' he asked.

'And sake.'

The beers came, ice-cold and delicious. A chef appeared behind the counter and, on a narrow plate, crisscrossed with hairline cracks, he began assembling a mountain range constructed of unfamiliar vegetables, golden filaments, and bulbs that resembled spring onions, all similarly arranged in little mounds.

'White radish, onions, roots, ginger, local sprouting vegetables,' Paul said when the chef placed his sculpture before them and a waitress brought bowls filled with a steaming broth, a dish of plump white noodles for each of them, and a little bowl with toasted sesame seeds and a wooden spoon.

He pointed at her bowl.

'You add three spoonfuls of sesame seeds, a few vegetables, some udon, you eat, and then you start again.'

The sake arrived, cold and exquisite. Rose sprinkled her sesame seeds into the broth, sensed how they trembled, and felt reinvigorated. She carefully added strands of ginger, radishes, and various sprouting vegetables, then tried to move some noodles to the broth, had to retrieve them clumsily from the wooden countertop, ended up grabbing one of them with her fingers, struggled some more, and stopped, breathless.

'Is this to wear the customer out before they even get started?' she asked.

She looked around, saw that the other diners lowered their faces right down to the bowl and noisily slurped up their noodles. She took the plunge and went after a noodle that slid like an eel through her chopsticks and fell back into the broth, splashing the front of her blouse.

'I get it. It's an initiation.'

He smiled. She tried something else with the next batch of noodles, sliding them from one bowl to the other, using her chopsticks sideways like tongs.

'I ran into the Englishwoman from the Silver Pavilion in town,' she said. 'She knew Haru.'

He raised an intrigued eyebrow.

'An older woman, very distinguished?'

'Yes, and she speaks perfect French.'

'Beth Scott,' he said. 'An old friend. She learned of your existence at the funeral, along with half the town.'

Rose put her chopsticks down.

'No one knew?'

'Almost no one.'

'Who did know?'

'Sayoko and I.'

'Who else?'

'No one.'

'Not even your wife?'

'My wife is dead,' he said.

There was a silence. She wanted to say, *I'm so sorry*, and couldn't.

'Was she Japanese?' she asked.

'She was Belgian, like me.'

He put his chopsticks down and took a sip of beer.

'When did she die?' asked Rose.

'Eight years ago.'

She thought: his daughter is motherless. In the silence broken only by sips of beer, somewhere in a tenuous, immense place, as invisible as the sky, something changed position. She could sense rain coming, a smell of thirsty soil, grass in the wind. There was yet another shift, a scent of undergrowth and moss. She began to weep, huge sobs, tears of sparkling pearls. She could feel them forming, flowing, and bursting into the world, adorned with light. She hated herself. Head down, she went on sobbing. Her nose was running. Paul handed her a tissue. She took it, sobbed even harder. He said nothing, calmly finishing his beer. She was grateful to him for that, the flood abated, she regained her self-control.

'I'll take you for a drink,' he said, standing up.

The darkness in the car was a balm to Rose. The tears and the sake gave a texture to the city, the patina of a mercury mirror.

'What was the hardest thing?' she asked.

He didn't answer; she thought she must have been indiscreet.

'I'm sorry,' she said, 'that was indiscreet of me.'

He shook his head.

'I'm looking for the right words.'

His voice was distant, muffled.

'The absence, initially,' he continued. 'And then, the duty, the cross to bear, to be happy without Clara.'

'Duty?' echoed Rose. 'For your daughter's sake?'

'No,' he said, 'for mine.'

Perturbed, she said nothing.

'You feel as if you no longer speak the same language as other people,' he continued. 'And you realise it's the language of love.'

'I've never spoken it,' she said.

'What makes you think that?'

'I don't believe you can give when you've never received, any

51

more than I believe your empty phrases about giving making you come alive. Otherwise, what would be the point of giving once you're dead?'

'You're beginning to understand the nature of his sacrifice,' he replied.

'This is all a pointless farce,' she declared.

The car stopped in a small street in the centre of town. They went up an outdoor staircase to the top floor of a drab little concrete building and entered a room with large picture windows that looked out on the mountains of the East. A bar ran the length of the room, but the decor, with its sand-coated walls and light oak furniture, was overshadowed by the splendour of the mountains, open to a night of mysteries, to the dark poem of the ridges. They were alone. As they were taking their seats, a young Japanese woman emerged from a hidden door on the right.

'Sake?' Paul asked Rose.

She nodded.

'I feel like drinking,' she said.

'You're not the only one.'

She was grateful to him for this unexpected complicity and relaxed. After the first, silent round of sake, he ordered another, and she felt like talking.

'Where's your daughter?'

'On Sadogashima, in the Sea of Japan, with a friend,' he replied. 'They wander about all day long; she told me today that she left her bento in her bicycle basket and a crow attacked it, but she was mostly outraged that no one had thought to make a bento for the crow.'

The tenderness of his voice, the images, the story about the crow, all of it seemed irritating to Rose.

'Why did you study Japanese?'

'Because Clara was studying it.'

She felt suddenly sober, wanted to say something to go back to feeling drunk, but the door opencd, and someone came in, yelling. Paul turned around and smiled. The elderly Japanese man, as wrinkled as a tortoise, was dead drunk. He was wearing a sort of herringbone fedora, crushed on top. One shirt tail was hanging out, and his linen jacket had been through the wars. When he saw Rose and Paul, he raised his arms merrily to the heavens and fell flat on the floor. Paul obligingly helped him to his feet, while he let out a torrent of joyful words and eventually made his way to the bar.

'Keisuke Shibata, painter, poet, calligrapher, and potter,' Paul told Rose.

And lush, thought Rose. Keisuke Shibata bent over and peered up at her from below, blowing his sake breath in her face. Paul gently pulled him back and sat him down on a stool.

'He only speaks Japanese,' said Paul.

'Thank God,' said Rose.

Keisuke burped conscientiously.

'It shouldn't be too difficult to translate,' she said.

'Alas,' said Paul, 'he's an incorrigible chatterbox.'

And indeed, he began to chatter like a magpie, at times addressing Paul, at other times some invisible presence in the room. Rose emptied a few cups of sake. The old man babbled on as he drank. Paul replied in monosyllables and from time to time gave a laugh. Finally, the conversation slowed while the drunkard, his hands flat on the bar, whistled quietly to himself.

'Is he ever sober?' Rose asked.

'Sometimes.'

'What's his story?'

'He was born in Hiroshima in 1945. His family was obliterated by the bomb. In 1975, he lost his wife and daughter to an earthquake. In 1985, his eldest son was killed in a diving accident. On 11 March 2011, his other son, a biologist, was on a mission to Miyagi Prefecture on the coast, twenty kilometres from Sendai. He didn't have time to get to higher ground.'

With her nail, she scratched at an invisible spot on the bar. Something, somewhere, was threatening. She drank some more sake.

'It was raining the day Nobu's ashes were interred at the cemetery, and Keisuke collapsed in the mud by his tomb. Haru helped him up and held him close until the end of the ceremony. Someone came over with an umbrella, but he sent them away. They stood there together, motionless, in the rain, and gradually, one after the other, we closed our umbrellas. I remember feeling how heavy, how strong the rain was, then forgetting about it. We'd entered a world of ghosts. Our flesh was gone.'

He stopped talking, and Rose's feet suddenly felt cold. She tried to cling to the black sky, the kindly mountains. Menace was all around. She glimpsed shadows, a sudden downpour, foam on the ground. No, she thought forcefully – but rain was falling and she was on her knees, there were no more mountains, no more people, and in this world devoid of flesh, this abyss of closed umbrellas, she was foundering in the mud while all the cemeteries gathered together, and she merely drifted from one to the next, doomed to a fall, to the mire, to the floods.

'As I looked at Haru and Keisuke, knowing I'd be returning before long to that same cemetery, I thought: We are all prisoners of the furnaces of hell,' Paul said.

Next to him, the Japanese poet burped.

'It was raining on the day of my grandmother's funeral, too,' Rose said. 'I don't remember any mud, only rain. Everyone says I'm mad, but I could swear the rain was black.'

She paused, tried to gather her thoughts, gave up on any effort at coherence.

'Later I read that after the bombs, a black rain fell on Hiroshima and Nagasaki.'

She tried again to follow a thread that was eluding her.

'My grandmother loved irises. She loved it when it rained in the garden,' she said, thinking, I'm completely drunk.

Suddenly, in her mind's eye, she saw Paule's smiling face. She heard her say, *It's time to divide the irises*, saw her again in a white dress, leaning gracefully over the flowers, full of silence and love.

Next to them, Keisuke was saying something.

'He's asking who you are,' Paul said.

'And who am I?' asked Rose.

There was a brief exchange in Japanese, and Keisuke, mocking, tapped Paul on the shoulder.

'He says you look even more dead than your father,' Paul translated.

'Charming,' she murmured.

'Completely frozen,' he specified.

Keisuke laughed, twittered on as he looked at her.

'He thinks it's good karma, that you have to die a first time in order to be truly born.'

'Does he get his pronouncements from fortune cookies?' she asked.

Paul translated, and Keisuke clapped his hands.

'He says you don't know who you are.'

Then Keisuke pounded hard on the bar and cried, 'Ha!'

'He says it's normal, because you haven't been born yet.'

'And when will I be born, according to the Great Boozer in the Sky?'

'I'm not Buddha, you can bloody well figure it out yourself,' Paul translated, while Keisuke collapsed onto the bar, farting noisily, and started to snore, his head on his arms.

She turned to the picture windows. In the starry night, the mountains of the East, sleeping giants under a shroud of ink, spoke a familiar language. Somewhere inside Rose a spring was bubbling, but she knew she could hear and feel because she was drunk, and that the poems and the clear, flowing water would be gone by morning.

'What is it you like about Japan?' she asked.

There was a silence, then Paul said: 'The poetry and the clear-sighted drunkards.'

'That's enough to live on?'

As he was getting to his feet, without replying, she imagined that he meant to say: There is only love and then, death – but he'd held back because she was already dead. Later, during the night, Rose woke up. It was hot. Through the window, through the motionless tree branches, she saw the moon, huge and golden, and she recalled her dream. Sitting in a field of wild irises, looking straight at her, was a fox.

5

During the era of the samurai, on the island of Sado in the Sea of Japan, there lived a hermit who, from morning to night, gazed out at the horizon. He had taken a vow to devote his life to this contemplation, to allow himself to be entirely absorbed by it, to learn the intoxication of being nothing more than a line between the sea and the sky. However, as he always positioned himself behind a pine tree that prevented him from having an unobstructed view, he was asked why he did this, and he replied: Because there is nothing I fear more than success.

Behind a Pine Tree

In the morning it was raining. The mountains of the East steamed with mist rising into a diaphanous sky; the river was silenced by the downpour. In the pale morning, in the unfathomable grey, ghost-travelled landscape, sky and water fused and were consumed by the same ending. Rose was tortured by this emptiness yet could not break free of it; in the furnaces of hell, people closed their umbrellas; blind to her own life, she wandered through terrain as empty and barren as death. You never leave a battle front like this, she thought; you can't fight against something that has no substance. The previous day's carnations had been exchanged for a handful of irises in an eggshell-white vase. The sight of the flowers distracted her from the rain; she had her shower, got dressed, went into the maple room. For a moment it seemed to her that its branches were forming a cross, and stark against a dark sky she saw the crucifixes of places and times whose memory she despised. Then the vision faded, and the tree sparkled. She could no longer see the wayside cross in it, and she liked the fact that it was sprinkled with crystal-clear drops that stayed there, transparent and trembling. After a moment, she was surprised to see she was alone, and, suddenly, the thought of her father in the cemetery made her go outside. The humidity enveloped her like a tight kimono.

She went back in and found Sayoko wearing a dress and a raincoat, her hair loose, a handbag over her arm.

'Breakfast soon,' Sayoko said.

She vanished. After a moment, a phone rang, and after another short while, she reappeared with the usual tray.

'Paul-san meet you at temple,' she said. 'Today very busy. When Rose-san finish, drive with Kanto-san.'

This is like the army, thought Rose petulantly. The day's fish gave her some difficulty, the tea exasperated her. She got up, went to the door where Sayoko had vanished, and opened it.

'Could I get some coffee?' she asked.

In a room with sand-coated walls, a cast-iron teapot hung from the ceiling on a chain concealed inside a long bamboo cane, and dangled above the hearth, which was a simple square hole where heat rose from embers closely packed on the ashes. A tripod straddled the central area of the hearth, the entire set-up in the middle of a raised area of tatamis. All around, the walls were covered with shelving for dishes. Further along, under the window, there was a sink, then a water heater, soft stone worktops, and cupboards of light wood. Finally, hanging on the wall was an India ink calligraphy piece that flooded the space with its splashes like comets. The teapot was whistling, the room evoked forgotten feelings, a familiar elsewhere where Rose was getting lost. In her beige cotton dress with a band around her hair, Sayoko seemed younger, slightly vulnerable, and Rose wondered what her story was – was she married, how long had she been working for her father.

'I prepare coffee,' Sayoko said.

Rose nodded her thanks, was about to close the door again.

'Monsoon is here,' added Sayoko. 'I give you an umbrella later.'

That's all I need, thought Rose, the monsoon.

Then, on impulse, she said: 'You take care of people.'

Sayoko smiled. On her light, smooth face, a flower bloomed. Terrified, Rose hastily withdrew. I'm losing my mind, she thought, but she couldn't get away from the vision of the spreading corolla.

She pressed her forehead against the cold windowpane; rain was falling, the maple was dripping on the moss; Sayoko's smile was making her drift off course, to an elsewhere that murmured she was home.

Rose left the rest of her breakfast, avoided Sayoko's gaze, drank her coffee. At the door to the garden, Sayoko brought her a transparent umbrella. Rose opened it and liked the way she could see the world through the raindrops. In the car, the drive seemed to take a very long time, first west then north, until they reached a vast parking area outside a high enclosure with a huge wooden gate. Paul-san coming soon, said the driver. Rose-san waiting inside or outside? Outside, she said. The sound of rain on her umbrella did her good; for a moment she dreamed of living inside a full, enclosed raindrop, with no elsewhere and no past history, no prospects and no desire. She went up to the gate; on the other side, a path of stones threaded its way among temple walls; she turned back. After a few minutes, a taxi stopped next to her, and Paul got out, carrying a transparent umbrella.

'Forgive me,' he said, 'I had an important sale this morning.'

He opened his umbrella; a stray leaf landed on it.

'Have you already had a walk around?'

'No,' she said. 'Where are we?'

'At Daitoku-ji,' he replied, 'a complex of Zen Buddhist temples.'

'What for you is an important sale?' she asked, as they walked down the path to where it curved right. 'A lot of money?'

'A long-term client,' he said.

'What did you sell?'

'A screen. A big screen by one of the most famous living artists in Japan.'

'What did it cost?'

'Twenty million yen.'

'I can see you're not troubled by cash flow issues.'

'Or rather you're not,' he said.

She stopped in the middle of the path.

'I don't want any money.'

He stopped, too.

'You have no idea what you want.'

She could detect neither judgement nor reproach in his voice, and wanted to answer, but only made a gesture that meant, I've had enough of this. They went on walking.

'Why do you limp?' she asked.

'A climbing accident.'

It had stopped raining. She became aware of the pervasive silence, a *horizontal* silence, pure and incomprehensible – it makes no sense, she thought. And yet the silence hovered over the pathways, and she felt she was slicing through it just below hip level, that it was creating a layer of invisible waves between stone and air. On either side of the path there were walls, grey roofs, gardens visible through wooden entrances. She tried to keep in mind that she was merely a puppet, traipsing around according to the will of a dead man, but the silence of the place streamed over her, cast her loose among strange thoughts.

They stopped outside the entrance to a temple. On the right, on a wooden sign, she read *Kōtō-in*. Ahead, along a short, paved path, bamboo guardrails and pines gave way to ochre walls; further along on the left was the arch of a big gate with grey roof tiles. From what was obviously only an antechamber, there came the new feeling of a frontier, a fragrance from another world.

Rose set off down the path.

The music of the pine trees enveloped her like a liturgy, surrounded her with thorny, twisting branches that tapered into supple needles; a hymn-like atmosphere hovered in the air, the world grew sharper, she felt herself losing all sense of time. It began to rain again, a fine, even rain, so she opened her transparent umbrella – somewhere on the edge of her vision, something stirred. They went through the gate; there was another turn to the right and then, ahead of them, a walkway. Long and narrow, lined with camellia bushes and bamboo handrails above a silvery moss, surrounded, to the rear, by tall grey bamboo and overhung by an arch of maples, the path led to a gate with a roof of thatch and moss, beneath which irises grew amid a lacework of wilting leaves. In reality it was more than a mere path; this is a journey, thought Rose, one that leads to the end or the beginning. They carried on, and, as on the first day, she was overcome by an ancient sorrow that was bathed in bursts of joy, drawn from nowhere. After two more bends they reached the entrance to the temple. Walking down the corridors to a gallery that overlooked a wide expanse of moss, Rose felt at home. There was more bamboo here, more maple, a stone lantern, but above all a type of freedom, an open arrangement where thatch and trees seemed to play in the wind. She breathed lightly, overcome with a sensation of *possibility*, swept away towards a delightful vanishing point – freer, imperfect, and alive.

Bowls of frothy green tea were brought; she peered at the tea, doubtfully.

'Matcha,' said Paul, looking at her.

Then, as she was hesitating: 'Go on, life's about trying new things.'

Reluctantly, she lifted the bowl to her lips. In the taste of greenery, the onslaught of leaves and grass, of duckweed and watercress, she recognised the land of rice and mountains to which she had been brought – a land where salt and sugar had been removed from everything, leaving only a blandness, a taste of nothing, a smooth, pale concentrate of the forest from a time before humans lived there. The taste of nothing, the taste of everything, she thought. This country's killing me.

'This country's killing me,' she said.

He laughed, and she didn't know whether it meant he agreed or was mocking her. She tried to define the drifting sensation she felt.

'It's something to do with childhood,' she added.

'You don't like that?' he asked.

'I don't see that there's anything good about childhood.'

'But it's not something you can just forget about.'

'So that's your constant argument, that it's there, so we just have to live with it?' she said.

'It doesn't mean resignation. I'm just trying to understand what is defeat and what is wisdom.'

'Defeat?' she asked. 'If there's defeat, where's the victory?'

He looked about him.

'Life is transformation. These gardens are melancholy transformed into joy, pain transmuted into pleasure. What you see here is hell turned into beauty.'

'No one lives in a Zen garden,' she retorted.

They left the temple by the path of wonders and found themselves once more in the antechamber of pine trees. She remembered the gardens at the Silver Pavilion, pruned to perfection with the sharpness of a sword, and those they had just visited, supple and carefree, at Kōtō-in – then she recalled that she had walked through those first gardens, too, as if they were a childhood land, and understood that each garden had its own share of innocence and precision, that they walked there together on the roof of hell admiring the trees, that this pendulum swing between the candour of happiness and the cruelty of desire was life itself. She stayed for a moment gazing at the pine trees. It began to rain harder, and they opened their umbrellas.

Later, the driver dropped them off at one end of the bridge she had walked across the day before. It had stopped raining, and Paul leaned for a moment on the railing to look at the mountains of the North. Navy blue against the dark grey of the sky, they sent powerful bursts of vapour up into the invisible vault. Crowds passed behind them – young people on a day out, tourists, ordinary men and women going about their business in a life that Rose found inaccessible and cruel. A solemn-looking *maiko* went by.

'The Sanjo bridge always grinds my heart,' Paul said, following the *maiko* with his gaze.

Rose observed the woman's white neck, imagined a life of secrets, of weeping in the night.

'Not my words, Keisuke's,' he added.

> the Sanjo bridge always grinds my heart
> like a tender grain of rice and changes it
> into flour on the neck of a maiko

She followed him to the same shopping street she'd been to, but this time they turned left and entered a restaurant with a long counter of light wood. Paul greeted the waitress and walked through to a room at the back containing a single large table. The light enfolded them in a silky breath of air; Rose saw the light and felt the breath on her skin at the same time. During the lunch, consisting of a succession of strange, fiddly little dishes, they did not speak. At the end, Paul ordered coffee, and she felt like talking.

'That tea this morning had almost no taste, and yet it tasted of everything,' she ventured.

'That's a good definition of Japan,' he said.

She pursued her thought.

'My grandmother said that everything seemed to crush my mother, that she viewed life as a single block of granite, one overwhelming mass.'

'There is a property belonging to the imperial estate, to the west of the city, known as the Villa Katsura.'

He fell silent.

'And?' she said.

He didn't answer. He was thinking.

'At the entrance, the view of the garden and the ponds is blocked by a pine tree in such a way that you can't take it all in at once,' he continued. 'Maybe life is no more than a picture you can see from behind a tree. We are offered life as a whole, but we can only see it through a succession of viewpoints. Depression makes you blind to perspectives. Life as a whole crushes you.'

She banished from her mind the images that were rushing in, and focused on the trees of Kōtō-in, on the setting of moss and foliage where a lantern had dropped anchor; she lost herself in the branches, attentive to their calligraphy, their unspoken text. They are prisoners of the earth, she thought, and yet they are the possibility of life, pruned to speak of roots and of flight, of great weight and lightness, of the power of our acts, despite our prisons. Then her gloomy mood got the upper hand again.

'Life always ends up crushing us,' she said. 'What's the point of trying, since we're in prison?'

'Where's the risk?' he asked. 'The mere fact of being alive means that all the risks have already been taken.'

Alone again in her father's house, she wandered idly between her room and the maple room. The doors along the corridor were inviting, but whenever she reached out towards one of them, she was seized by a feeling of sacrilege. The recollection of the *maiko*'s grave expression made her go and sit opposite the tree in its glass cage. Her thoughts drifted; time went by with glacial stillness. I'm afraid, she thought suddenly, and an image came out of nowhere. When? she wondered, seeing again the fresh corolla placed next to a botanical map with hazy edges. The hawthorn petals were vibrating gently, she saw herself taking a few notes; the scene vanished; somewhere inside her, the flower was fluttering. *I was studying, I was learning my trade.* She tried to recall the moment, then was struck by the pointlessness of her endeavour and, with it, of any endeavour. And so the image yielded to yet another, and behind the torn screen of memory, her mother's smiling face appeared to her. In her shaky recollection her mother seemed more real, more truly herself than in the past, and the irony of such an incarnation drew a harsh laugh from Rose. How many smiles had there been in thirty-five years? she thought, bitterly, and everything came back all at once – Paule's kitchen, the flower and the map on the table, Maud standing before her, luminous, all shadows flown, smiling and saying, Is that a hawthorn? How old was I? thought Rose. Twenty? A hundred, for sure. And then: What is the hardest kind of mourning? When you mourn for what you've lost, or for what you've never had? Then, suddenly, she thought of the pine tree at the Villa Katsura that prevented you from seeing all of life, and again she told herself: I'm not afraid of failing, I'm afraid of success.

6

There is in Kyōto an ordinary temple that has none of the beauty of the city's great jewels, but it is much loved for its plot of two thousand plum trees, and the entire city goes for walks there during the final days of February. And yet Issa, the magnificent poet, only went there when the wood of the trees was still black and barren, devoid of the flowers that would later fill the surroundings with fragrance. The moment the first corolla appeared, Issa left the plot, while his peers came to admire the miracle of petals cast along the wintry branches. If, now and again, someone showed concern regarding this inclination that robbed him of the loveliest show of blooms all year, he would laugh and say: I have waited a long time in a state of deprivation; now the plum blossom is inside me.

The Plum Blossom Is Inside Me

Maud, Rose's mother, had grown up in a state of melancholy, and no matter what she did later in life, she held fast to it, with admirable perseverance. Time washed life with rain and brought sunshine, the moon glowed, and Maud remained in darkness. What's more, she inhabited her sorrow the way a fox inhabits its den; when she emerged into the woods, it was only to retreat, unchanged, into her burrow; despite Paule's best efforts, Maud would always wash up against hard stone cliffs. After a certain amount of time, Paule gave up, broken-hearted and tired of trying. The years passed, heavy with cloud cover; Maud worked, travelled, came home, unchangeable in her sorrowful castle. And so when she returned from Kyōto bearing the child of a man she had left behind, Paule was overwhelmed. She wanted Maud to promise that the infant would know her father, and she came up against a rage the likes of which she'd never seen, the only ripple her daughter had ever made on the still sea of her melancholy.

Rose was born, and owed her name to Paule, who loved flowers and wanted her granddaughter to spend time with them. Before long, Maud stopped working and spent her days in the living room, facing the conservatory, ignoring the lilacs. From time to time she wept but, as with everything, with little conviction – so Paule would take Rose out into the garden, not imagining she might actually be able to protect her. For ten years, however, Paule held her breath and dared believe in the miracle: in fact, Rose was a charming child, who read, was curious, laughed all day long. Then, one evening, after a decade of not hearing her mother's tears, Rose, too, was devastated by them. To a certain Haru Ueno, whose name and address were on a letter to Maud, Paule sent the last photograph she had of Rose from before everything suddenly changed. On the back she simply signed *Paule*, and never found out whether he'd received the letter, or been tempted to reply, to overstep the bounds; for a long time this haunted her.

In his letter to Maud, Haru Ueno wrote only: *I will respect your wish, I will not try to see my daughter, don't worry.* One day, when Rose was celebrating her twentieth birthday, Paule realised she must have read it. When? she asked, but she knew the answer. You said nothing about it for ten years? she added. Rose nodded and they spoke no more of it for another decade and a half. That year, one evening in June, Maud went to the river with her pockets full of stones and drowned in magnificent silence, after admiring the trees in the mirror of calm water.

'All that for this?' Rose said angrily.

'Now you can meet your father,' murmured Paule.

'I could have met him sooner,' answered Rose. 'The letter wasn't for me.'

Then their lives were once again deafened by silence. Two years later, it was Paule's turn to die. That same evening, Rose made love with her current beau with such cruel indifference that she did not feel him withdraw from her, did not hear him leave the room, did not remember, the next day, having had him in her bed, in her body, in her now-bloodless life. A few months went by where she did not recognise herself any more. A sort of relief came from defeat, and she stopped trying to be happy; her desire to be happy was already so tenuous, and had been for so long, that it gave up, indolently. Three years drifted by in this shapeless lethargy. Finally, she took a plane to Kyōto.

She woke up to a feeling of rain and misfortune. The sound of the falling water made the world seem evanescent, distant. She went to the maple room, found it bathed in a strange brightness. A fragment of joy burst from this darkness shimmering with rain.

Sayoko emerged from the kitchen.

'Paul-san coming,' she said. 'Rose-san want tea?'

'Coffee, please,' she replied.

She would have liked to keep her there, ask her who she was, why she spoke English. The Japanese woman sensed her hesitation, and stood there for a moment, but as Rose didn't say anything, she went away. She came back with an irregularly shaped red cup, as delicate as a poppy, and looked at Rose as she drank.

'Rose-san beautiful,' she said.

Surprised, Rose put her cup down.

'Japanese people always find Western people beautiful,' she said.

Sayoko laughed.

'Not always. Too fat.'

They heard the hall door slide open.

'I remember your mother,' said Sayoko. 'Very sad.'

Finally, when Paul entered the room, she slipped away.

'Where are we going today?' asked Rose.

'Shinnyo-dō.'

'Let me guess: a Buddhist temple?'

'A Buddhist temple.'

In the car, she felt as if her life were following the vanishing lines of the grey streets.

'Will it rain for long?' she asked.

'For a while, but you'll miss the cool monsoon air when the summer heat begins.'

'Not a great climate you've got here.'

'You get used to it.'

'Japan, the country where they suffer a great deal and don't seem to mind,' she recalled.

He seemed surprised.

'That's what your friend Beth Scott told me the first day.'

'Beth has a romantic vision of Japan,' said Paul. 'She's one of those people who live in a Zen garden.'

The car stopped next to a stone walkway that led to a red gate then climbed up to a temple and a pagoda of dark wood. It had stopped raining, they did not take their umbrellas, and they stepped out of the car into a fragrance of damp earth and unfamiliar flowers. Rose started up the walkway, then turned around, sensing a presence. There was no one. Further along, the great courtyard of the temple was deserted, but the sensation grew stronger. *We are not alone here.* Because of these silent, invisible beings she knew nothing about, whose presence draped the world in a new brilliance, she felt as if she were floating aimlessly through time. She looked around her at the maple trees, the wooden pagoda; she looked at the great dark temple perched on its solitary hill – without tourists, without visitors. Where did it come from, this feeling that they were not alone, that spirits surrounded them, leading them into secret hiding places? At the same time, she perceived something *mischievous*; nothing made sense, everything was saturated with sense; what is this place? she wondered.

'What is this place?' she said out loud.

'A temple where Haru used to come walking every week.'

'It's inhabited,' she said, aware she was talking nonsense.

'It's a place of the spirit.'

She was surprised by her own exasperated response.

'Don't you ever get tired of being so stuffy and solemn?'

For the first time since she'd met him he seemed annoyed.

'You leave me no room for anything else.'

'You're a dead man's flunky; that's what makes you so uptight and insipid,' she continued.

'I'm the executor of a man I admired, and in keeping with his request, I've been dragging his pain-in-the-arse of a daughter from one temple to the next. Is that what you want? You want me to join in with your depressive-aggressive little game?'

Leaving her there, he walked off to the right, around the temple, and disappeared from view. She stood there motionless for a moment, furious with herself for being so stupid, for having hurt him, relieved, too, that in the end he was simply ordinary. Great sage, my arse, she said out loud, and laughed. Knowing that she would apologise did her good. She was charmed by the mischief of the spirits of the place. What are you? she said, again, out loud. *Kami?* Ghosts? She followed the path Paul had taken, found herself behind the temple, beneath an impossibly graceful archway of maples, then turned right along high walls. Ahead of her in the distance she saw tombs – a cemetery, she thought, that's what was missing. She held her breath as she walked among the graves, the lanterns, the heavenly bamboo. There were stones shaped like faceless characters and long strips of wood clacking in the wind; decorated with tightly packed inscriptions, the strips surrounded the graves, narrow gravestones standing on simple marble plinths; some of them had been eroded by the years, invaded by lichen. On either side, seasonal flowers had been placed in tall vases of the same marble. Everywhere, the moss rippled, glinting tender, blue, everywhere the lanterns' winged hats added a playful note to the atmosphere. In that silence of the dead, life was extended, and sparkled at the same time. Tall evergreen trees rustled in the wind; something else, too, rustled in a glittering of unknown magic, in the craftsmanship of the tombs and temples, the clacking wood, the crows' cries. The birds circled slowly above the roofs, and Rose liked their dissonant call – close to breaking, she thought, and yet so calm. Then: what a place. She continued on her way and saw that she was now at the top of a hill. To the right stretched the city in its basin. At the end of the path, sitting on the top step of a long stairway that led down to other tombs and other temples, Paul was waiting for her, gazing out at Kyōto. She sat down next to him.

'I'm sorry,' she said.

'You're not sorry,' he fired back. 'You're a professional pain in the arse.' He laughed. 'That's absolutely fine by me; I'm tired of being understanding,' he added.

On the far side of the city, slightly dimmed in the gathering dusk, the mountains of the West glistened faintly. From the clouds a dark, electric light fell; varnished with rain, the temple roofs gleamed like watered silk. At the day's end, Rose was no longer shocked by the ugliness of the modern city. There were no skyscrapers to be seen, the stark outlines of concrete had been smudged into a drab whole. Paul stood up, and she followed him down the steps. The wind had dropped, it was warm and humid, she felt herself descending past a row of spirits, past years that had fled, leaving no memory behind. Near the bottom they turned left onto a short path that ended behind a temple. Paul stopped next to a tomb.

'This is Kurodani,' he said, 'with Clara's ashes, and Keisuke's son Nobu's, and Haru's.'

She gazed at her father's tomb.

'What am I supposed to feel?' she asked.

'I have no idea,' he replied.

She looked up at the top of the stairway.

'This place is extraordinary, but I don't know why,' she said.

Something inside her fluttered like a dragonfly. The ineffable presences, the heavenly bamboo, and the gaiety of the stones had a powerful effect, and for a moment she felt dizzy. She was startled by a stray gust of wind amid the calm of evening, and she shivered. The tomb did not speak to her but seemed to cast invisible fish hooks to lodge in her, and although it was subtle, she detected a change in the banality of the moment – nothing spectacular, she thought, unless I'm growing gills. Abruptly, she fell to her knees and, with the flat of her hand, touched the damp earth by the grave.

Matter. Here lies my father, she thought. She stood up. Everything was identical; everything had *mutated.* She felt drained, exhausted. She looked at Paul. He was weeping.

There was a brief rain shower as they left and headed down a silent street to where Kanto was waiting for them by the car, in the dark. Rose felt intoxicated by an awareness of the earth, space had expanded, the air was scented with violets. Paul said nothing, but between them there was a new intimacy – it's better than sex, she thought. In the car, she took his hand briefly. He squeezed it, did not look at her.

At the restaurant, a sort of bar where people drank and nibbled on little fried meat skewers, they were silent for a moment. The half-light in the place gave objects and faces a warm, slightly shifting iridescence. In a lighted alcove, luminous specks danced on an arrangement of bare branches. The sake deepened their intimacy, Rose felt light, gently tipsy without being drunk.

'No flowers,' she said, pointing to the vase in the alcove.

'Plum tree branches,' he said. 'The Japanese like them even better than cherry trees.'

'But it's not the season.'

'It might be a tribute to Issa. He only walked among the plum trees before they bloomed, and when they asked him why, he would say, The blossom is inside me.'

She took a sip of the ice-cold, almost white sake.

'The cemetery wasn't on the agenda today,' she said.

He put his cup down, looked at her thoughtfully.

'It was not one of Haru's requests,' she added.

'I don't go to Kurodani often,' he said eventually. 'When I'm there, I'm not thinking about my dead, I'm thinking about their funerals.'

My dead, she repeated inwardly. Do I have anyone I can refer to as *my dead?*

'The hardest thing, it turns out, is not trying to be happy without the person you loved,' he continued. 'It's changing, no longer being who you were with that person.'

'Do you feel as if you're betraying your wife?' Rose asked.

'I feel like I'm betraying myself,' he replied.

They left the restaurant as the sky cleared briefly. In the open bowl of clouds, an enormous moon was shining, faintly reddish.

'We're not that far from the house,' he said. 'Would you like to walk?'

He sent Kanto home, and they walked along the river, on the moonlit banks, brushing past tall grasses that bent and stretched like ballerinas. They passed a few people out strolling, their faces blanched by the moon; it was chilly, Paul gave her his jacket. He was lost in thought; she continued walking, filled with elation. The cemetery was speaking to her, her father's tomb was calling to her, inside her she felt the workings of death, without it being a burden; now these workings took the form of a circle dance where cheerful spirits stepped in, uncertain and familiar silhouettes; the memory of the deserted temple was veiled in a silver film, the invisible presences only gaining their true shape in hindsight. Devils, she murmured, oh merry devils, come to me the way you used to – and she smiled at this sudden recollection of long-ago fairy tales. They arrived at the house, and by the sliding door Paul said goodnight. She would have liked to keep him there; he took a step back, smiled at her. The moon disappeared behind a cloud, she couldn't see him any more, she heard him close the gate and walk away, his footsteps calm and uneven .

During the night, she dreamed she was walking with her father through a field of plum trees near a dark wooden temple. Walking behind them were the devils from her childhood fairy tales. Stopping by an extremely beautiful flower, with petals sparkling like diamonds, stamens like lines of clear ink, Haru held out his hand to her and said: You will risk suffering, giving, the unknown, love, failure and great change. And so, just as the plum blossom is in me, my entire life will pass into you.

—

gazing at flowers

7

During the era of the great shoguns, towards the end of medieval times, there came a winter so harsh that the rivers of the archipelago froze over, and animals could no longer drink from the streams. One morning in February, on leaving his house, a little boy came upon a ferret. Are you thirsty? he asked it after a tender look had passed between them. The ferret inclined its snout, and the boy led it over to a clump of violets that had broken through the ice during the night. There he said, Drink from the flowers, and the ferret licked the tiny purple stems avidly. What do we know about this little boy today? Not much, to be honest – but we do know that he became one of the founders of the Way of Tea, and that one day he composed a poem that spoke of violets in the ice.

Violets in the Ice

R ose awoke and looked out of the window. The slopes were bathed in thick mist that rose in successive exhalations towards a transparent sky. It had stopped raining; the river gave off a heavy scent of earth. Paul, she thought, then: Everything slips through my fingers.

In the maple room, Sayoko brought her breakfast, wearing a black kimono decorated with wisteria blossoms.

'Paul-san in Tōkyō today,' she said. 'Rose-san go to temple with Kanto-san.'

'In Tōkyō?' she asked. 'It was planned?'

'Very important client,' said Sayoko.

'When will he be back?'

'Day after tomorrow.'

Left by the wayside, thought Rose. The cawing of a crow outside exasperated her; impatient, she stood up, went to her bedroom, and came back with Beth Scott's business card.

'Can you call her?' she asked.

The crystal clarity of Sayoko's clipped sentences only increased her frustration; she reached brusquely for the receiver.

'Do you have some time today?' she asked the Englishwoman.

'This afternoon,' Beth replied. 'I'll tell Sayoko where we can meet.'

Sayoko took the telephone, listened, and hung up, with an imperceptible pout of disapproval. She doesn't like her, thought Rose, with spiteful satisfaction.

'I won't go to the temple,' she said.

'Yes, you go,' said Sayoko placidly.

Rose felt like saying *go to hell*, thought better of it, went out, crossed the garden, where the rain-blemished azaleas looked wretched to her, then got in the car, slamming the door. During the drive towards the mountains of the East she looked only at her hands. When Kanto stopped and said, This is Nanzen-ji, she got out, slamming the door again, took a few enraged steps, stumbled. Behind her, Kanto added, Temple there. She turned around and saw that he was pointing right to the end of a tree-lined path.

It was an extraordinary place – temples everywhere, trees, moss, tall gates with curved wings. She walked to a huge gate with two roof levels, one storey of paper partitions, and a cap of grey tiles. Through it, maple branches were visible, and, in the distance, in front of a temple, was a huge incense holder from which pale curls of smoke rose up. It was windy, and you could hear the clicking of the invisible bamboo; the air smelled of rain. She climbed the steps that led to a gate with two large rectangular openings, supported by gigantic pillars. She went through it and felt as if she had passed through an invisible screen, then strode up the path to the bronze basin. The incense made the world thick; walking through the layers of scent, she could feel it leaving its mark on her. Turning right, she reached the main walkway and followed it to the entrance of Nanzen-ji. Kanto showed up behind her, paid for her admission, handed her a piece of paper, and went off again. She was surprised by the whiteness of the outside walls, as well as the semi-darkness of the wooden inner galleries. As she passed through this gloomy prologue and re-entered the light, something gripped her by the throat. *For the first time I can see.* She sat on the floor, stayed there gazing at the rectangle of sand and foliage. All around ran inner galleries, then walls topped by grey tiles. At the front, grey sand had been raked into parallel lines, both straight and curved. At the back, in front of the wall, four trees made music, lapped by a sea of moss, ancient stones, and a few azalea shrubs. It was the most sober, most oddly *outdated* garden she had ever seen, as if it had returned from a journey through geological eons, and yet, everything about it was alive – stillness in motion, she thought, limpid and vibrant, the absolute presence of things, the final lesson of the world. How many centuries to arrive at this absolute present? She looked up and saw sand, moss, trees, walls, and tiles superimposed on each other; beyond them, the trees clung to the hillside, set out like sculptures, reaching out towards the ink of the sky; she saw the living spirit of architecture, its changing, perfect nature – she said it out loud: perfect. She thought of Paul and felt a pang in her heart. After a moment, she strode through the other galleries, found the adjacent gardens ordinary, came back to the initial tableau, and lost herself in it again. Leaving was an exquisite, wrenching moment. I will come back, she said, again out loud.

She found Kanto out in the little car park; she felt new, elemental. He locked the car, pointed to the street below and said, Going to eat now. Eat what? she asked. Tofu, he replied. She followed him past little temples fronted by tiny gardens with trees that looked hand-drawn. Further on, on the left, they went through a gate and down an alleyway which had maple trees and moss on one side, and on the other a large hall filled with tatami mats that could be seen through slightly blurry windowpanes. They were asked to remove their shoes and then invited to sit on cushions at a table with a little stove. Only one menu, said Kanto. She bit into a cube of tofu brushed with green sauce, was surprised by the flavour of soy sauce and an unfamiliar herb, and laughed for no reason; Kanto remained impassive; again they were served a toasted tea when she would have preferred a beer. Meet Scott-san now, he said. She followed him out to the car, watched the streets rush by without seeing them, gave a start when Kanto came to open her door. Scott-san inside, he said, pointing to an entrance hidden by short curtains.

Nanzen-ji was still having an effect on her, and she felt as if she were wrapped in a veil of mineral substance, where something was drifting off course, something was turning liquid. She entered the tea house through a glass door hidden behind four cloth hangings printed with ideograms. It was an old building with dark walls and a roof and awning covered with grey tiles; inside was a dream of wood, worn shelves holding ancient jars of tea sealed with orange cords ending in long tassels; a press of young women in light blouses, green aprons, and white scarves that looked like nuns' wimples greeted her enthusiastically. Straight ahead there were signs hanging from the ceiling, probably indicating the various teas available. An L-shaped counter closed off the space. At the back, a tall calligraphy banner hung over the aisles where employees were busy weighing and wrapping. On the right, an illuminated glass cabinet displayed utensils, boxes of tea, and a precious little jar whose price seemed exorbitant to Rose. She jumped when someone came to speak to her in English. Close up, the young woman's headscarf distracted her, and she didn't understand what she was saying.

'*Okyakusama* needs help?' said the young woman again.

'Oh,' said Rose. 'The tea room, please?'

The young woman smiled, pointed to the back of the shop, and motioned to her to turn right. Beth Scott was waiting for her, reading, her back against the sand-finished wall. The tables were made of the same old, dark wood that gave the house its patina. Slatted partitions of a lighter wood added a contemporary note. Oddly enough, the conjunction of these more modern elements and the cast-iron kettle and bamboo utensils behind the counter made it seem to Rose as if time were being extended, and fervour

83

lost. On one side the street was visible through a window identical to the ones in her bedroom; on the other side, the glass panes of a picture window opened onto a miniature tableau of plant life, with a maple tree, a fern, and a few azaleas.

Beth Scott looked up at Rose.

'Oh, hello, hello,' she said. 'I'm so glad to see you again.'

And as Rose was taking her seat: 'Ready for a mystical experience?'

In the dim light, her face was soft, almost silky.

'Where are we?' Rose asked.

'In the only tea house in town that serves *koicha*.'

They examined each other.

'You've come a long way,' said the Englishwoman.

A waitress came over, and Beth ordered, delighting Rose with her way of speaking Japanese. The young woman in her green apron laughed, putting her hand in front of her mouth, then slipped away, shuffling her feet along the floor.

'I've just come from Nanzen-ji,' Rose said. 'My father is having me dragged around from one temple to the next; I suppose that counts as coming a long way.'

'Nanzen-ji isn't the most beautiful,' Beth said, 'but it always makes me want to cry.'

'I've heard you spend all your time in Zen gardens,' Rose said.

'Did Paul say that?' she asked with a laugh.

Rose blushed at hearing Paul's name.

'How did you know my father?'

'I was one of his clients, but we were friends as well.'

'What do you do in life?'

'Various things. I'm a widow, I have money, I love Kyōto, I live here nine months of the year – what else is there to say?'

There are plenty of other things to say, thought Rose.

'My mother died five years ago,' she said. 'At the time I thought my father would get in touch with me.'

'Five years ago?' Beth repeated. 'Haru fell ill five years ago, and after that his illness was long and cruel.'

'Everyone here has been ill,' said Rose.

'Are you thinking of Clara?' Beth asked.

The waitress set a little oblong green cake down in front of Beth, with a pink and white one for Rose and, in lieu of forks, little bamboo sticks. Rose's plate was streaked with brown and grey lines.

'Eat,' said Beth. 'It's better to have something in your stomach.'

Rose struggled with her little stick, hindered by the soft texture of the cake. Inside was a red paste, sweet on the tongue, exquisitely contrasting with the sugary blandness of the outside.

'What was she like?' Rose asked.

'Clara? Funny, pragmatic, no-nonsense. Paul is secretive, a complex personality. She was his access to life on earth. They laughed a lot together. She loved him very much.'

Rose put down her little stick.

'Paul has spent this last decade looking after sick people,' said Beth. 'He lived exclusively for them, for his daughter, and for his work.'

'There haven't been any women in his life since Clara died?'

'There have been women, but I wouldn't say they're in his life.'

'Women in Tōkyō? asked Rose, and immediately regretted it.

The tone of Beth Scott's reply was neutral.

'They're not important.'

I don't need anyone else's help to make myself look ridiculous, thought Rose, exasperated.

'Clara's funeral was the saddest I've ever been to,' Beth continued. 'Anna was two years old; Paul could only keep going because she was there. Without her, I think he would have died. He was in hell, and we were at his side, so sorry for him, unable to help.'

Rose had a sudden intuition.

'Why does he limp?' she asked.

'That's up to him to tell you,' Beth replied.

The waitress brought two bowls on a tray, which she set down on the next table. She turned the first bowl in her palm, placed it in front of Beth, and bowed. It was a lovely pale brown colour, decorated with a tastefully executed white rabbit. Rose liked it, but the other bowl enthralled her – its irregularities, grey crackling on a clear glaze, its tortured sobriety, the impertinence of its bold scars.

'This technique of crazed firing comes from the Northern Song Dynasty,' Beth said. 'Isn't it magnificent? From the utmost simplicity, totally unexpectedly, complexity is born.'

Inside each bowl there was a sort of bright green, almost fluorescent paste. Rose tilted her bowl back and forth. The paste hardly moved.

'You drink this?' she asked.

Beth nodded. Rose breathed in the substance, and she recalled the tea at Kōtō-in, the strength that came from nothing, its total power; she drank as if plunging into cold water. The bitterness grabbed her in the stomach and then, immediately afterwards, her mouth was filled with a taste of watercress, vegetable, prairie grass – do I like this? she wondered. Everything became sharper. An awareness of vast green expanses ran down her throat.

'This is the first concentrated matcha of the tea ceremony,' Beth said. 'Now they will serve you a second, lighter one, adding water to what remains inside the bowl.'

Rose licked what she could of the remaining tea paste. Something drew her back to Nanzen-ji, to the density of time, to a lost sense of the primitive. The waitress came to collect the bowls. Rose didn't want any more cake, nothing but the intense bitterness and its offer of a journey to a forgotten land.

'Last night I dreamed of a large temple with a field of plum trees in front of it,' she said.

'That could be Kitano Tenmangū,' said Beth, 'on Imadegawa, to the west. In February, everyone goes there to admire the flowers.'

She pointed to her bowl.

'At the end of the sixteenth century, they had one of the greatest tea ceremonies ever organised for the emperor, with three of the founders of the Way of Tea, including Sen no Rikyū. There were said to be thousands of guests.'

All of a sudden, Rose thought of Paul. She shook her head, tried to distract herself.

'Do you have children?' she asked.

Beth ignored her question.

'The revelation of your existence came as a shock,' she said. 'Just imagine half of Kyōto at the funeral, and Paul reading Haru's letter.'

'Letter?' said Rose.

Silence.

'I think the lawyer will pass it on to you,' Beth said, finally.

'Everything is being decided without me,' Rose murmured.

Beth laughed.

'That's life.'

A second tea was brought, with the same taste as the one at Kōtō-in but finer; in it, Rose could make out the scents of the forest, of trampled undergrowth.

'What did you like about Nanzen-ji?' Beth asked.

Rose searched for the right words.

'Something clear, primitive, liquid yet unmoving.'

Beth laughed again, appreciatively, but somewhat surprised.

'You two are alike, Paul and you,' she said.

'I don't see how,' Rose said.

'The sea inside you. That's where you sail.'

Beth tilted her head thoughtfully.

'Haru would have liked that,' she added.

She hadn't touched her cake.

'Would you like it?' she asked.

Rose shook her head. Beth smiled.

'I've got to go now,' she said, 'but next time I'll take you to another tea house I think you'll also like.'

They parted in the street. Back at Haru's, Rose lay on the futon, feeling unbearably tense – or is this frustration? she wondered. The irises from the day before had been replaced by a pink camellia, and she was struck by its resonance with Nanzen-ji. It's all connected, she thought, but I'm not part of that *all*. Again she saw the still yet moving stones, the lined grey sand, the trees on the moss; every image reminded her of Paul's absence; not knowing why, she could feel great ice floes drifting, liquid shards. After an hour of this shapeless idleness, she stood up, went out into the corridor, stood still, waiting. Finally she turned left, and, by the dark wooden panels, she slid open a door at random. She entered a cool, bare room. Scattered on the tatami mats were bowls for tea, a few earthenware and lacquer containers, and a little bamboo whisk. On the floor was a brazier topped by a cast-iron kettle; in an alcove, a scroll portraying three violets bending towards an icy ground; below it, in a bronze vase, a little piece of bamboo. Through the picture window that opened onto a patio of azaleas, she saw the dying day cast a pearly sheen over the damp leaves. The room was empty, silent – and yet Rose could sense *something living*, an attentive, silent ghost. She went over to a brown bowl with uneven sides, tried to imagine her father in this room, using these utensils, drinking from these superb, humble bowls. Next to the bamboo whisk, a sort of shiny handkerchief had been forgotten: a deep, lovely violet, it lay there in languid folds, as if it had just been dropped by an invisible hand, and, for a moment, Rose thought she caught a glimpse of a bending figure, moving slowly, with delicate yet lively gestures. She stood before the scroll in the alcove. Below the flowers, calligraphy characters had been set out as if for a poem. A few of them, on the top right-hand side, seemed to morph into birds, soaring up towards the sky; a light mist rose from the frozen ground; the violets *were alive*. A noise outside roused her from her meditation. She went out and closed the door, stirred by a strange reverence.

In the maple room, she found Sayoko sitting at a low table, papers spread out before her, glasses on her nose.

'I'd like to go to Kitsune for dinner,' Rose said.

'Now?' asked Sayoko.

She nodded. Sayoko took out her phone, called someone, hung up.

'Kanto-san coming in ten minutes.'

'Thank you,' said Rose.

And, on impulse: 'I need to write a letter.'

Sayoko got to her feet and went over to a little desk to fetch a sheet of paper and an envelope. Rose sat down next to her, took the pen Sayoko held out to her, and let her mind wander at random. Then she wrote: *I would like you to tell me about my father.* Finally, holding her breath: *I miss you.* She folded the paper quickly, sealed the envelope, and handed it to Sayoko, saying, For Paul; then, appalled, she fled into the garden.

8

During the Northern Song Dynasty in China, when poetry, painting, and calligraphy developed in unison, tucked like jewels in the dreams of ancient wise men, there was a particular fondness for representing and versifying flowers and landscapes. One of the greatest landscape artists of that era had a granddaughter who would beg him every day to draw her a camellia. For an entire decade, she pleaded on behalf of her flower. At the age of fifteen, she died one night from a galloping affliction. At dawn, Fan Kuan painted a camellia damp with his tears, and beneath it he inscribed a poem of petals flown away. Finally, gazing at the still-damp scroll, he saw, to his terror, that it was his finest work.

A Camellia Damp with His Tears

As they were pulling up next to Kitsune's red lantern, she no longer knew why she had wanted to come. Kanto sat at the bar; she sat opposite, at a table for six. The yakitori restaurant was deserted. The chef came to see her. Same as last time but beer only, she said. He returned to his stove. He'd shown no emotion. She drank her first beer in one go and looked around her. She saw new details. On the counter, in front of the sake bottles, was an old rotary telephone; enamelled advertising signs were diligently rusting away; some of the manga posters were torn. What sort of man had Haru been, to enjoy coming to a place like this? she wondered. A wave of resentment swept over her and she ordered another beer. She felt lonely and blind, blamed herself for being too sentimental, and hated herself for having hoped – for what? she thought, ordering a third beer. Kanto had his back to her, was placidly talking to the chef; she could sense his respectful vigilance, and found it aggravating. The workings of death, the workings of the liquid stones, the letter she had written to Paul – all seemed ridiculous to her now. She nibbled on her meat skewers with the same resentment. When she asked for a fourth beer, she saw the chef glance at Kanto. The driver made a little gesture that meant, I'll deal with it, and she was mortified. Later, when she wanted to get up, he came and held her by the shoulders. She did not protest, just let herself be led to the car. In the little garden, she motioned to him that she would walk on by herself; he didn't insist on helping her. She found herself in the darkened maple room; it was gently vibrating, the branches heavy with night; the trees of Nanzen-ji, painful and sharp, gripped her memory. She went to her room, got undressed. Naked, raw, she looked out of the window, ran her hand over her brow, noticed a piece of paper on the futon. She deciphered it in the dark, on her knees. *Paul-san coming tomorrow at 7:30. I wake you at 7:00, Sayoko.*

She fell onto the tatami, arms outstretched. A ladleful of stars shone through the clouds; from the river came a strange monotonous chant; she was awake for a long time, not moving. Some time later she awoke, shivering, dragged herself onto her futon, wrapped herself in the light sheet. It was a bright night; she felt the presence of secret spirits, of a life of semi-darkness heaving with sighs; she recalled her arrival, the magnolia flowers splattered with light, the presence, even then, of spirits. Everything is the same, everything is changing, she thought. A corolla was expanding, she felt terrified. She drifted off into a dreamless sleep. Three short knocks on her door startled her awake. She sat up and saw it was light outside. She had a splitting headache. It's seven o'clock, came Sayoko's voice on the other side of the door. I'm getting ready, mumbled Rose. She mistook the soap for the shampoo, couldn't do her hair, put on a crumpled dress, swapped it for a skirt and blouse that didn't go together. In the mirror she looked like an unfinished thing. She put on some lipstick, hastily scrubbed it off with cotton wool, went to the maple room. Paul and Sayoko looked at her and laughed. She stood still, nonplussed.

'What's wrong?' she asked.

Sayoko took three short steps over to her, removed a handkerchief from her sky-blue obi, and wiped Rose's cheek. Rose met her gaze, read discreet compassion in her expression. Sayoko took a step back, considered her work, laughed again, and pointed to her blouse.

'You've put it on inside out,' said Paul. 'Is it a new fashion? Is it meant to go with the lipstick on your cheek?'

He was smiling. He looked tired, amused. She told herself that he was tall, with a fair complexion – tall and tired, she thought, I'm wearing him out.

'Do I have time to get changed?' she asked.

'It would be a pity; you've already lit up my dreary day.'

'I've got a really bad headache,' she said.

He said a few words to Sayoko, who motioned Rose to follow her into the kitchen. There she sat her down like a child, handed her a glass of water and a white tablet, which Rose swallowed obediently. Rose-san eat something? asked Sayoko. She declined, put her blouse on the right way, left the kitchen, and followed Paul to the entrance. They went through the garden. By the gate, she turned and saw Sayoko bow, then give them a little wave. Rose lowered her head and climbed into the car.

'Forgive me for getting you up so early,' said Paul, 'but we need to be at the temple when it opens. After that it really will get too busy.'

'I thought you were staying in Tōkyō today,' she said.

'I got back early this morning. After dinner, I stopped by the flat, had a shower, and caught the 4 a.m. Shinkansen.'

'You have a flat in Tōkyō?'

'It's Haru's.'

'You didn't get any sleep?'

'No,' he said. 'I was having dinner with clients. A very long dinner.'

He laughed.

'No serious transactions are ever made in Japan without a long dinner and a great deal of sake.'

She wondered if he'd received her letter, imagined him on a station platform, lost in his thoughts without a single one for her. His presence next to her was disturbing; she remembered taking his hand, two days ago; now the thought of it horrified her. He didn't say anything, watched the streets fly past. The car stopped in a car park already crowded with three coachloads of visitors. She followed him down a long leafy walkway lined with little shops, waited for him by the ticket office, fell in behind him along a path that went past a large pond with lily pads that seemed unpleasantly picturesque to her – this is a tourist trap, she thought, then: I'm a load of dirty washing being carted around from one laundry to the next. They left the pond's edge, climbed a few stone steps beneath an archway of indolent maples, came to the entrance of the temple, removed their shoes, turned left behind other visitors, and there was the garden before them.

'Ryōan-ji,' Paul said.

She looked at the large rectangle of stones and sand and felt nothing. And then, as if suddenly overwhelmed, she let herself slip to the floor of the wooden gallery, crushed by *matter*. Maple and cherry branches cascaded down the walls of the enclosure from outside the garden. Beyond, the foliage formed a bushy, exuberant screen. Inside, there was just sand streaked with parallel lines and seven stones of differing sizes, ellipses raked around them – but Rose was only looking at the walls with their sloping roofs, grey ridge tiles, and bark surface. Ochre and moiré, with the patina of an Italian palazzo, they reflected the gold of the layers of moss surrounding the stones.

'Have the walls always been this colour?' she asked.

'No,' Paul said. 'I think they were white, originally.'

'They make the garden,' she said.

He seemed surprised.

'The stones have been set out in such a way that you can never see all of them at once,' he said.

She tried to concentrate on the rocks and the sand, but her mind strayed, returning to the fresco of the walls.

'There's no end of commentary on Ryōan-ji,' he added.

'Have you read it?'

'Some of it, for work.'

'And did you learn anything?'

'Did you learn anything from reading your books on botany?' he asked.

She didn't like the question.

'I suppose so,' she said.

And yet I'm not looking at the flowers, she thought. In search of consolation, she went back to the *matter*.

'Haru was a tough businessman, and a loyal friend,' Paul said.

He got my note, she thought. Something reeled inside her, the substance of the walls caught her.

'When I met him, he said: I have a great deal of taste but no talent. Over the years I understood that this was his strength: he knew exactly who he was.'

She tried to concentrate on the ellipses around the first three stones, couldn't focus her attention.

'That is what drew so many people to him.'

Rose let her gaze return to the golden walls.

'He was Japanese in his habits but unconventional in his thoughts. I believe he also liked to have me around because he needed a foreign listener, who would be receptive to unorthodox ideas.'

'About what?'

'About women, for example. Japanese women have not had a feminist movement like ours, but Haru was a feminist, in his way. He didn't just invite men to his parties. He was interested in what women had to say.'

'Is that why he had kids from casual affairs with foreign women?' she asked, and, knowing this was childish of her, bit her lip.

He said nothing.

'His finest character trait was that he knew how to give. Most people give in order to receive, out of a sense of duty, or because it's the done thing, a sort of automatic reflex. But Haru gave because he understood the significance of giving.'

She got a whiff of something like danger; she stared at the wall, and her gaze was suddenly drawn to a stone. Almost level with the sand, smaller than the others, it was sailing across a boundless sea.

'Those last months, when Clara was very ill, Haru and I would talk every evening. I'd come and see him in his study, we'd drink sake, he listened and talked to me. I never got the feeling that it was an effort for him. I don't know if two men have ever had a closer friendship.'

He fell silent, and she understood that he didn't want to go on. Behind them, a troop of noisy Chinese visitors made the gallery floor tremble.

'Ryōan-ji doesn't inspire you?' he asked.

'It looks like a giant cat litter tray.'

He burst out laughing and, for a split second, was transformed. That's the old Paul, she thought, the Paul that was killed off by his wife's death. They stayed there for a moment in silence. Reading a text of rock and sand, Rose let her gaze wander from the stone that had first caught her eye to the others; the scene, too, was transformed; she studied the walls, no longer saw there what she thought she had seen. She went back to the dryness of the rectangle of sand, detected a vibration in *time* – time of birth, time of suffering, time of death, she thought. She looked at Paul. He had closed his eyes, and she recalled his tears at the cemetery. The sense of danger was growing, at the same time as a friendly presence, a quiver of hope. And so, looking at the walls that time had turned ochre, she knew they only remained standing thanks to the strength of the garden, that its flowerless mineral nature transformed time into eternity, and that, through this metamorphosis, no action could ever have the same significance; finally, for some unknown reason, the way Sayoko had waved earlier came back to her – in the solitude of the stones lost in sand, there was a gift. What gift? she wondered, examining the scene. What can such dry, bare space give? She let her spirit wander with the music the seven stones played, again felt they were drowning her in a timeless ocean, and that the garden, by itself, *was giving*.

Paul got up, and she followed, focusing on his uneven, flowing gait. In the car, she could see that he was tired.

'And now?' she asked.

'I'm taking you back to Haru's.'

'We're not having lunch together?'

'I have to go and get Anna; she came back last night,' he said.

'You came back for Anna?' she asked.

He didn't seem to have heard.

'And for the last temple visits before the lawyer visit, of course,' she added.

'I came back for you,' he said. 'I was missing my professional pain in the arse.'

He leaned towards Kanto, said something to which the driver nodded, then made a short phone call in Japanese. The drive took a long time, in a silence that made her feel fragile. In the centre of town, on a wide street with arcades, they got out of the car. Paul slipped through an entrance, climbed a flight of stairs. She could sense how tired he was, the pain in his hip. He opened a door, and they were in an ultra-modern room with white tables and apple-green chairs. Behind the counter, large posters depicted waffles with an extravagant variety of toppings. He sat down with relief, and she took the chair opposite him.

'Waffles?' she asked.

'Don't forget I *am* Belgian.'

The door opened behind her. He smiled and stood up, full of energy again. Rose turned to see a suntanned little girl hurrying towards them. She paused briefly on noticing Rose, then threw herself into her father's arms. She was accompanied by a Japanese woman who must have been in her forties and who came forward shyly. With his arm around his daughter's shoulders, Paul greeted her, and they exchanged a few words with a laugh. Rose had stood up. Anna's face fascinated her.

'Anna, this is Rose,' Paul said.

The girl looked at her with a serious expression, came closer, stood on tiptoe, and kissed her on the cheek.

'Are you Harū's daughter?' she asked.

'So it seems,' replied Rose.

Anna studied her intensely, her mouth closed, her brow creased.

'Rose, I'd like to introduce Megumi,' said Paul, 'the mother of Anna's friend Yoko.'

The Japanese woman bowed, gave a smile, and said a few hesitant words.

'She welcomes you to Kyōto. She asks how long you are planning to stay.'

'I don't know,' said Rose. 'I'm doing as I'm told.'

Again, Anna's sharp gaze. Paul translated something that seemed to satisfy Megumi; she took leave of them with a bow; at the door, she turned and made the same gesture as Sayoko. The waitress came to take their order, Anna began chattering, and Paul listened, smiling. The waffles arrived, the little girl pounced on hers, while Rose gazed warily at her own construction of pastry, green coulis and red grains.

'Don't you like waffles?' Anna asked, her mouth full.

'I'm not sure I like the look of this weird green concoction from Mars,' she answered.

The little girl burst out laughing and looked at her father. Rose was surprised to see that she was so dark and olive-skinned where he was blond and pale; she was also small and delicate, with fine features, her nose slightly upturned, her eyes dark and shining. She must be the spitting image of her mother, thought Rose. Between voracious mouthfuls, Anna told them about her holidays, laughed, occasionally stared at Rose; and Rose sensed her vigilance, her patient, meticulous watchfulness; I used to be like that, she recalled. Anna begged Paul to order another waffle, looked to Rose for support, beamed with triumph when he gave in. Then suddenly she turned serious.

'Where do you live?' she asked.

'In Paris,' answered Rose, 'but I also have a house in Touraine.'

'Where's that?'

'A little bit further south.'

'Do they have stories there?'

'Stories?'

'Stories about the fairies and sprites that live there?'

The little girl was looking her in the eye. Do I want to be any part of this? wondered Rose. She looked at Paul. The furrow in his brow had deepened; she saw that he was concerned. Anna was waiting.

'Yes,' she said finally. 'My grandmother knew all of them, particularly the ones about merry devils.'

'Will you tell me them?' asked Anna.

Rose's heart, tugged at like a weed, was for a split second between two worlds; then the stones of Ryōan-ji entered the circle dance – their starkness, their stony solitude, the certainty of their unspoken text: everything was laid bare. Something shifted, and she felt a sharp pain.

'I'll tell you all of them,' she said.

Anna smiled at her. I'm a butterfly being pinned alive, thought Rose. Paul stood up and went to pay. She could tell he was relieved. Kanto was waiting for them at the foot of the stairs.

'You're off duty now,' Paul said to her. 'I have to go with Anna to the dentist, and then I've got to take some clients out to dinner. I'll come for you tomorrow morning; Kanto is at your disposal today.'

'And you?' she asked.

'I live just nearby,' he said, pointing to the buildings in the city centre. 'Where do you want to go?'

'I have to go back and get changed first.'

He said a few words to Kanto, she got in the car, Anna leaned over and kissed her on the cheek again. Rose met Paul's gaze and saw a shadow of sadness. She would have liked to take his arm, keep him there, pull him towards her. He closed the door. As the car was pulling away, Anna waved her hand energetically, and

Rose answered with the same gesture Sayoko had made. When they got to Haru's, she went up to her room, dropped to the floor, and spent the rest of the morning there. The pink camellia was resplendent with jaunty and melancholy flames, and she was drawn into a contemplative mood, something inside her stirring relentlessly.

Later, she got changed, went to the deserted maple room, knocked on the door to the kitchen, and went in. Sayoko and a young woman in a housecoat were drinking tea. They made her coffee and a bowl of rice, and she waited, sitting on the tatami. The two women were having an animated conversation, and Rose listened, relieved not to have to speak, glad she didn't understand. She drank her coffee, ate the rice, wanted to leave. Sayoko motioned her to wait, rummaged in her handbag, which was on a shelf, took out a phone, and handed it to her. Code zero zero zero zero, she said. Number one is Paul-san, number two is Sayoko, number three is Kanto-san. Rose took the phone, went back up to her room and lay down again. A massive downpour was turning the world dark, the camellia shone in flashes with the shimmering of the rain. After a while, Rose went out, and, in the corridor, on impulse, she opened the sliding door that was opposite the tea room. She went into a tatami room that looked out on the river. The only furnishing was a hospital bed, poised in the space like a spider; a large abstract painting hung opposite; a black vase stood on a lacquered night table. In the rain-light, the scene seemed to be in motion, uncertain. In response to the pale stain of the mattress, the painting exuded a vibrant power, an immense carmine stain drowning in a flat tint of deep ink. But although it had neither features nor contours, Rose was convinced it represented a flower: a camellia, a lotus, perhaps a rose. Did he die here? she wondered and, going closer, she reached out to touch the bare mattress. She held her breath, hesitated, stepped back. An indefinable scent combining cedar, aniseed, and violet drifted through the room. Shadows seemed to linger there, and for a moment she thought she could feel a breath on the back of her neck. The harshness of the metal bed unsettled her, just as another sensation was working its way through her. Suddenly, she was seized by the absolute certainty that the corolla *was alive*, despite the power of death. She thought of Anna, her shining eyes, the merry devils, the wave she'd given her as the car was pulling away. And then again she saw the garden of sand and stone, surrounded by walls of gold, and thought: The walls are nothing without the garden; our time on earth is nothing without the eternity of giving.

9

We are told that one morning, Sen no Rikyū was washing the stones on the path to his tea house with clear water when a young fox emerged from the nearby trees and stopped to wait under the foliage of a tall heavenly bamboo. After a moment during which they observed each other in silence, the little fox carefully tore off a branch of bamboo and went to leave it on a flat stone where the guests for that evening's ceremony would be sure to step. When his young disciple expressed his surprise that his master had left it there, in the way of the guests, Sen no Rikyū said to him: The fox and the bamboo teach us to take a different path.

The Bamboo Teaches Us to Take a Different Path

A t three o'clock, Rose decided to go out. In the maple room, she found Sayoko busy arranging a cluster of magnolia branches. She explained that she was going out, but Sayoko left her flowers, went to fetch a little purse with a pattern of pink clouds from a low table, and handed it to her, saying, Money for stroll. Rose thanked her with a wave of her hand, Sayoko smiled, and she smiled back, uncertainly. As she was about to turn and leave, Sayoko took a photograph from her belt and held it out to her. Surprised, Rose took it. It was of Sayoko and three other women with the same gentle face; the only difference was the colour and cut of their grey or black hair; each one had pearly skin, a pure oval face; they were laughing, sitting on tatami mats in front of a mountain setting.

'My sisters,' Sayoko said.

Rose was speechless. The print was creased; she imagined Sayoko must look at it often. Curious, she studied the sisters' features. Dutiful women, she thought, but their laughter is lively.

'You need one,' Sayoko added.

Rose nodded, handed back the photograph. In the hall, she reached for an umbrella. It was raining, steady showers, but the sky had lightened, and the sun was visible through the cut-out clouds. She went to the river; motionless herons stood guard, scattered along the banks. She walked as far as the bridge from the second day, turned left in front of the entrance to the covered gallery, walked for a while under the arcades on the street where the waffle restaurant was. An automatic door opened on her right, letting out an insanely loud din from inside. She went into a vast room with harsh neon lights, did not understand what she was looking at. Men and women sat staring vacantly at multicoloured slot machines. The noise was unbelievable, the ugliness indescribable; this, she thought, is hell, the real hell, Haru's anti-world. She fled the absurdity of this mad Japan, and made her way back to the covered gallery, turned right towards the main road, crossed it, and continued north. A few metres on, the street regained some charm, lined with elegant boutiques. She went into one, admired the ceramics displayed on wooden shelves, bowls like her father's; it was all magnificent. Closing in on a shallow bowl that had the grainy texture of rice, white with irregular patches that intermittently caught the light, she saw next to it a photo of a man in front of a potter's wheel. She wondered if he was one of Haru's artists, worked out the price of the piece, decided it wasn't expensive enough. She went back out, up the street, looking in the windows at brushes, paper, lacquer. She felt incongruous, at a loose end; Kyōto wasn't expecting her, didn't know her, she was wandering aimlessly, feeling useless and futile. She thought of Sayoko, of the four sisters, their smiling faces – trapped but still radiant, she mused, and she felt more out of place than ever. Before long, on the right, she recognised the tea house from the fluttering banners with their ideograms. Everything that had previously seemed graceless here in the town centre touched her now – the little buildings, the peaceful streets, the smart boutiques – she understood at last how they were a continuation of those wonderful gardens. Beth Scott's words came back to her: gardens where gods come for tea. A country for merry devils, more like, she thought; even at the heart of the sublime, you're in the company of the child you used to be.

She went into the tea house, and was led to a table on the other side of the room. She ordered in English, and saw the waitress in the green apron smile. Which *koicha?* asked the young woman. Rose was flustered. She was shown the menu, there were two sorts, she chose the least expensive. Taking a thick gulp, she thought of Paul, his absence, his profound sadness. She couldn't stand the thought that she would have to wait until tomorrow to see him again. I'm a pile of dirty laundry left on the empty counter, she thought again. She took another gulp of *koicha*, and suddenly all she was aware of was Anna's face – her attentive eyes, eager for stories of sprites, the thought that she didn't have her father's features, that she looked like her mother. Rose finished her bowl, waited for the next one, drank quickly, comforted by the pleasant, lighter tea. She took out the phone Sayoko had given her, struggled for a moment with the keys, found the contacts, pressed the third one, and waited. When she heard Kanto's voice, she said, I am at the tea house, can you come? Ten minutes, he replied. She paid and went out to wait on the pavement. It had stopped raining, the air smelled of tar.

Kanto arrived and turned to her once she was in the car. Can we go to Nanzen-ji? she asked. Closed now, he replied. She looked at her phone. It was six o'clock. Home then, she said. In the deserted maple room, an urge came over her to lie down and sleep beneath the foliage. She gave a start when her phone rang. She opened it, saw *Paul* on the screen. She answered, her heart pounding.

'Are you too tired for a drink after dinner?' she heard him ask.
'No,' she replied.
'Will you be in town?'
'I'll be at Haru's.'
'I'll come by for you as soon as I've finished with my clients.'

She went to her room, took a bath, put on a floral dress, lipstick, pinned up her hair, resisted the impulse to remove her make-up, went back to the big room. The maple was swaying slightly. She lay down on a low sofa and enjoyed the sensation of capsizing.

Before long, she fell asleep. In the depths of her hazy dreams, a fairy was flying, a fairy with Anna's face; she glided across the sky, then landed on Rose's shoulder and said her name. Rose woke up and, opening her eyes, saw Paul leaning over her. She sat up, disorientated. His gaze was kind, but then all of a sudden, he laughed.

'You clearly have a problem with lipstick,' he said.

She ran her hand over her cheek, and he laughed again.

'Maybe you should use a mirror,' he suggested.

She went into the bathroom and saw that lipstick had run down from the right-hand corner of her mouth. I was drooling, she thought, horrified. She removed her make-up, took a step towards the door, changed her mind, put some more lipstick on, and fixed her hair. Returning to Paul, she could tell from the way he looked at her that he thought she was beautiful. She followed him out to the car through the moist air, under a moon draped with mist. Someone called him on the phone, the conversation in Japanese lasted a long time; she could hear the weariness in his voice, could sense his reserve, the restraint in his body. He hung up; she couldn't stand the silence and squirmed in her seat.

'Have you ever thought of moving back to Belgium?' she asked.

He turned to her. In the gloom of the car, his face was serious, accentuating the line on his forehead. His pale skin was like a mask.

'Belgium?'

His phone rang again. He ignored it.

'All I wanted when I came to Japan was to live in Kyōto and be surrounded by a certain type of art and culture. Haru made that possible for me. Death has finally anchored me here.'

She wanted to change the subject and say, You haven't slept for two days, you must be exhausted, but the car was already pulling over on a street in the centre of town. They got out, went up a short flight of steps to an anonymous door, and entered a large, dark room lit in places by sparkling cones. Along the wall on the left, a line of heavenly bamboo burst from a bed of grey pebbles.

On the right, customers were drinking at a counter in front of sake cellars illuminated like chapels. Joyful cries greeted their entrance; from a table at the far end of the room, five men waved their arms at Rose and Paul, and Rose recognised one of them.

'The drunken potter,' she murmured.

'But with his gang, which is even more formidable,' said Paul. 'Sadly, there's no going back now.'

'Who are the others?'

'A photographer, a producer for national television, a musician, and a French colleague of mine, all of them well gone by this point.'

'A colleague?'

'A Parisian antique dealer, to be more precise.'

They approached the table, and Rose suddenly felt lighter. I'll have a drink, she thought – after all, why not? The Japanese men gazed at her kindly, there was a mocking smile on Keisuke Shibata's lips. Her eyes met his. This is the night for a showdown, she thought, surprised at this unlikely thought. The Frenchman, an unshaven man in his fifties wearing a cashmere sweater and a floppy polka-dot necktie, doffed an invisible hat.

'Are you French, Mademoiselle?' he asked.

She nodded. He let out a quiet whistle.

'Forgive me for not standing,' he said, 'but I'm not really up to it just now. As for my Japanese friends, they're all barbarians, they don't stand in the presence of women.'

He seemed to reflect for a moment.

'Although I am the only gay man here.'

Then, pouring himself another drink: 'Which has nothing to do with it.'

Rose and Paul sat down, the Japanese noisily called for more sake, Rose downed her first cup in one go.

'My name is Édouard,' said the antique dealer she had sat down next to. 'And you are?'

'Rose.'

Keisuke said her father's name with a chuckle.

'Oh, so you're Haru's daughter?'

'Among other things,' she replied.

'And otherwise?' he asked.

'I'm a botanist.'

'And apart from that?'

Apart from that? she wondered.

'I'm a pain in the arse.'

He laughed and began a conversation about everything and nothing, and, helped by the sake, she willingly joined in. The evening went on in this vein: she drank, she chatted with Édouard, she laughed, and, after an hour, she knew she was completely drunk. They seemed to her to have been talking about flowers, and restaurants, and love, and betrayal – but her gaze, for a while now, had kept returning to the heavenly bamboo, one branch of which, lower than the others, was brushing against the wooden floor; it looked like a rebellious feather on the smooth plumage of a pale green bird; having slipped out of place, now in the way, it was shouting something at the top of its chlorophyll lungs. Across from her, Paul was talking to the people on either side of him; at regular intervals, Keisuke shouted for more sake.

'What are they talking about?' she asked Édouard.

'Politics.'

The conversations gradually slowed. During a lull, Keisuke jerked his chin in her direction.

'He says you seem to have defrosted a little,' said Paul.

The poet was looking at her; she could read the irony in his eyes and, to her astonishment, immense kindness.

'He says you're pretty but you don't smile, as well as being too thin.'

The drunkard added a few words that made the others laugh.

'And what was that?' asked Rose.

'Something meant for me, which I won't be translating,' he replied.

In Japanese this time, Paul told a story in which she could clearly make out the name *Ryōan-ji*, and they all burst out laughing. Édouard patted her on the back.

'I shared with them that you compared Ryōan-ji to a giant litter tray,' said Paul.

Keisuke shouted something, banging on the table, and the guests agreed, nodding their heads in unison.

'Fucking Zen priests,' Paul translated.

The potter looked gloomy again.

'Ryōan-ji, the end of the world,' Paul translated.

Then, as no explanation followed, they all resumed their conversations, and Rose went back to chatting with Édouard. At one point, when Paul went over to say hello to some acquaintances near the door, she asked her new friend what it was Paul hadn't wanted to translate earlier on.

'Oh, happy to oblige,' he laughed. 'Keisuke said to him: You should fuck her nicely, that would properly defrost her.'

He looked at Paul.

'Personally, I wouldn't say no,' he added.

And, as Paul headed back to their table: 'I didn't tell you anything.'

There was another silence, and Keisuke pointed a finger at Rose. Ah, she thought, the showdown. He began speaking, and Paul got up and took a chair from the next table and sat behind Rose. He translated simultaneously; she could feel his breath on her neck.

'Your father was the spirit of a samurai in the body of a merchant, an exploitative bastard, but he paid well, and, above all, he was a loyal friend. Paul is cut from the same cloth, less brutal, but cleverer. And as he's Belgian, the Japanese don't see him coming. He learned from his master, he was his disciple, his confidant, his doctor, his friend.'

He paused. From time to time, Rose looked at the bamboo branch, behind the potter. She was struck by its lack of symmetry, its rebellious languor.

'Do you know what a friend is?' continued Keisuke.

'A dead man?' she suggested.

He laughed loudly when Paul translated.

'Your father said: it's someone you'd be happy to be shipwrecked with. Mountain people are very stupid, but when everything's collapsing around you, the only person you want by your side is an idiot like that. And you? Are you also as remarkable and stupid as that?'

'No,' she said, 'I'm French.'

He exploded with laughter.

'You really are your father's daughter,' he croaked.

Someone walked past the bamboo branch, making a detour around it, and Rose was enthralled. Keisuke asked Paul a question, and he answered with one word.

'Did you know your father liked flowers?' asked the drunkard. 'But you're an idiot botanist, you stick labels on them, so basically you don't give a damn.'

She looked him in the eye and saw only tenderness. For whom? she wondered. For him? For me?

'Your father, at least, knew how to look at them,' continued Keisuke.

'All the flowers except Rose,' she said.

He was following a train of thought and ignored her remark.

'Do you specialise in anything?'

'Botanical geography.'

'You follow the flower trail?' he asked.

'In a way.'

He giggled.

'It's about time you found them.'

He poured some more sake.

'*A single rose is every rose,*' he said. 'That's Rilke, nothing to do with your useless science. Do you think your father didn't look at roses? He lived his life as a merchant and never understood women at all, but he was a samurai, he knew that straight lines are fatal.'

Rose went back to the bamboo branch. Something was niggling

at the back of her mind, but kept slipping away, then returning.

'If straight lines are fatal to men, then why not to women?' Paul translated. 'If you don't understand that, you might as well go straight to hell.'

The potter snorted noisily, wiped his nose on the sleeve of his jacket.

'You're young, you can afford to take a different path. Afterwards, it will be too late.'

He seemed on the point of adding something, then gave up. He looked at Paul.

'You yourself know it very well, ashes, ashes . . .'

He suddenly looked tired, put his head in his hands, murmured a few words.

'What did he say?' Rose asked.

'After ashes, roses,' said Paul.

His voice was husky. I've turned up after the battle's over, she thought; they went through the end of the world together, I will never be part of that. Paul sat back down on the other side of the table; she felt abandoned.

'Does Keisuke say *tu* to me?' she asked Édouard.

'They don't really have *tu* and *vous* in Japanese the way we do in French, but he speaks to you the way he would if you were his daughter, with the informal pronouns that are the equivalent of saying *tu* in French.'

'As if I were his daughter?' she echoed. 'Now I've got a dead man and a drunk as potential fathers.'

'He lost all three of his children,' Édouard pointed out, kindly. 'You can't hold it against him for being daft enough to want to adopt a French pain in the arse.'

After a while, Paul stood up and bid the gathering goodbye. He seemed exhausted, and she followed him quietly. By the entrance, she stepped around the rebellious bamboo branch, and she got the distinct impression that she was taking a path she'd long known and long forgotten; she paused for a moment, struck by this detour to a place of no matter or substance. Outside, she took a deep breath. The air smelled of summer, Kanto was waiting for them, standing in the dark, silent, unreal. As she got into the car, she suddenly turned and found herself almost up against Paul. He was surprised, stepped back slightly. She felt drunk but oddly alert.

'Do you want to . . .' she murmured.

She put her hand on his forearm. He took her by the shoulders and propelled her gently into the car, like a child. She wanted so badly for him to want – for him to want what? Her mind was wandering.

'You've had more than enough to drink,' he said, 'and I'm not that sober myself.'

He leaned towards her.

'I'll pick you up tomorrow morning; we'll be going to another part of town. And after that to the lawyer's.'

'What's going to happen there?' she asked.

'He'll tell you what Haru has left you.'

She wanted to reply: What do I care what he's left me? But behind Paul, in the narrow view from the street to the river, she saw great bands of mist rising in the moonlight. She thought about her renegade bamboo, its determination to break away with all the vitality of a runaway – somewhere in her skull, Keisuke's voice was murmuring *different path*, and she heard herself say:

'I accept.'

Before he closed the door, she saw the flash of emotion on his face – the real Paul, she thought – then the car slipped away into the night. Going into Haru's house now felt like coming home. In her room, she made a vow to the mists rising up towards the mountains and the monsoon sky, towards the red moon. She fell asleep, a deep sleep, woke briefly, looked through the window for the moon and found it, huge and tawny, veined with dark branches.

10

At the very end of the Ming Dynasty, the future painter Shitao, then only three years old, lost his entire family, murdered by a rival faction in the court of the Chongzhen Emperor. A servant saved him from the massacre and led him to the Buddhist monks of Mount Xiang. There, he learned calligraphy. Later, he set out into the world to fulfil his destiny as an artist.

Shitao, a name that means *stone wave*, portrayed rocks in such a way that you would have sworn they were alive, but his true passion was moss. However, he never depicted it on his scrolls. One day, when his friend the painter Zhū Dā asked him why this was so, he replied: Moss caresses stone like a loving woman, and soon, perhaps, I will manage to paint it – and then, far from battle, I will make my art into a story about love.

Moss Caresses Stone

In the early morning, it was pouring with rain. The world was fading away, the river was vibrating. Rose knelt on the tatami and saw that a tray had been left there with a glass of water and a white tablet. She pictured Paul calling Sayoko, them talking about her and him leaving instructions. A wave of shapeless desire ran through her. She took the tablet, lay down. *He knew exactly who he was.* She tried to recall the conversation, its setting, its texture. How do you know who you are? she wondered. The walls of gold came back to her – the stones, their sudden presence, their silent offering. What was the name of that garden? Ryōan-ji, she recalled, with a sense of triumph. Then, bitterly: I don't exist, so I cannot know who I am.

She showered and got dressed; every movement was painful; she lay down again, waited for the headache to pass, and saw that the camellia was gone. A moment later, she went into the main room and found Sayoko, wearing the brown kimono from the first day, with her peony obi. Seated at a low table, she was writing in an accounts book. She got up, went into the kitchen, and reappeared with the morning tray. While Rose was struggling with an entire fish, Sayoko went on with her bookkeeping. The sound of rain on the moss around the maple was duller than usual. Rose finished her breakfast, thought of going out, changed her mind.

'No flowers in my room today?' she asked.

Sayoko smiled.

'Paul-san want you choose.'

Surprised, Rose remained silent. Sayoko studied her for a moment, in a serious and focused way.

'Paul-san secret man,' she said finally.

And as Rose looked at her, even more surprised: 'Very brave. He know flowers.'

What does that have to do with it? thought Rose. And me? Am I brave?

'Rose-san want which flower?' asked Sayoko.

She felt a bit lost.

'In France, I like lilac,' she said.

'We have lilac in Japan,' said Sayoko. *'Rairakku.* Good season now.'

They heard the front door slide open, and Paul came into the room; Rose took to heart his smiling face and thoughtful look; he is handsome, she thought. He said a few words to Sayoko, who left the room with hurried little steps.

'Were you able to get some rest?' he asked.

'Yes, but I've got a headache,' she replied. 'And you?'

'I slept like a log; I feel like a new man.'

Sayoko came back with coffee. Paul drank his slowly, while Sayoko spoke volubly to him and Rose waited, watching them, sensing an elusive life unfold inside her and then vanish. Finally, they looked at her, and Sayoko gave a little nod.

'Are you ready?' asked Paul. 'Today we have to keep to the schedule.'

In the car, his nearness unsettled her. He still seemed tired, a bit absent.

'Where are we going?' she asked.

'The other side of town, Arashiyama.'

'Does that mean something?'

'Storm mountain.'

'Which temple?'
'Saihō-ji.'

They drove a long way west, in silence, not looking at each other. The city changed, became dreary, impersonal, devoid of the charm of the centre; they went down streets full of anonymous buildings and ugly neon; the thought that all she'd seen of Japan was six temples and a cemetery upset her. Finally, they went down a narrow street, past tall bamboo plants, through an almost rural area. Other visitors were already waiting by the entrance. It was raining. After a few minutes, a monk in a black robe with a collar lined in white came to open the gate. Paul and the other visitors handed him a paper, and everyone followed him to the usual wooden buildings. They were led into a large hall with squat little lecterns where sheets of paper, ink, and brushes were laid out. Paul motioned Rose to stay at the back and take her place at one of the lecterns. She imitated her Japanese neighbour and sat on her heels, her toes turned slightly inwards. Paul folded his legs to one side, trying to hide a grimace. She studied the sheet in front of her, saw ideograms on it and wanted to ask for an explanation, but just then a procession of monks came in and headed to the centre of the hall. Speaking in laboured English, a surly-looking superior ordered the assembly to retrace, in ink, the characters of the sutra there before them. A young monk sat cross-legged in front of a little bench with a shiny black bowl on it; another sat by a sculpted wooden fish that rested on a large embroidered cushion. Both of them were holding a slim baton in their hand. Rose yawned.

The three crystal-clear chimes, the dull *pock*, got her in the guts. Sitting up straight, she saw that the first monk was holding his baton away from the shining bowl while the other monk was now tapping the wooden fish, keeping a rapid and regular rhythm. The chant began, a smell of incense rose, the voices were monotonous and fitful. The sound of the crystal bowl intermittently punctuated the recitation. The Japanese woman next to Rose was copying out her sutra, but Rose was caught up in a deep flow, intoxicated by a smell of damp earth mingled with dust and blossoms. At last, the monks fell silent. After a moment, during which the tall surly monk said something she did not understand, they were each given a little wooden plaque. The Japanese woman pointed to her brush and said to Rose, Write wish.

'What was that all about?' Rose asked Paul.

'*Hannya shingyō*, the sutra of the heart,' he replied.

'It's about love?'

'It's about emptiness.'

'The sutra of the heart is about emptiness?'

'The sutra of the heart of wisdom, yes.'

She laughed.

'For once I feel I'm where I belong,' she said.

He smiled and got to his feet, suppressing a grimace. They followed the stream of visitors outside to a gate in a wall, and once through it were told something else that Rose did not listen to. At last, they were free. A light drizzle was falling. The chant was still echoing inside her – the crystal-clear scansion, the muffled dullness. They went along a paved walkway that wound beneath a cloud of maple trees. This is undergrowth, she thought in astonishment. Rain filtered in scattered drops through the leaves; everywhere, extraordinary moss ruled supreme over its private kingdom; thick and undulating, covering root and stone, it seemed to glitter.

'The other name for Saihō-ji is Kokedera, the moss temple,' said Paul.

The moss is enchanted, she thought – or rather, the earth is, the earth beneath the moss.

'Haru believed that the earth of Kokedera was magical.'

'And you?' she asked, wishing she could say *tu* to him instead of *vous*.

He didn't answer. Then, as they came to a pond lost beneath the foliage: 'For me, this place is full of memories.'

Rose looked at the pond. A moss-covered bridge spanned it at a narrow point; a faint vapour skimmed the surface of the water; the shape of the banks spoke to her like writing.

'The humidity from the pond keeps the moss alive,' said Paul.

'It's an odd shape,' said Rose.

'People say it represents the ideogram for the heart.'

He raised his head, looked at the trees.

'That was our last carefree outing.'

A wave of sadness swept over Rose. I'm not mourning anyone, she thought. The dull crystal of the sutra continued to lull her like a melody being hummed far away. The moss glinted with drops of rain – monsoon dew, she thought. They continued along the path. Something was rising from the earth, she felt it brush against her, its secret magic.

'Anna was a year old; I was carrying her on my back,' said Paul.

'She says she remembers, but I don't see how she could.'

The merry devils, thought Rose. They walked on in silence. When they reached the end of the garden, she looked at the trees rooted in the sweep of velvet; looked at the raindrops, the kindness of water on plants and of plants on the earth; it's like a caress, she thought. The kinship of dew and moss, the fusion of crystal, earth, and wood suddenly made it absolutely clear to her that she had never stopped mourning Paule, that she had been mourning her for years, for silent centuries. She placed her hand on her heart, and then it was all over, in the scent of a cemetery, a psalm of black rain.

They left the temple and, after driving through countryside for a few kilometres, headed northwards along a river until they reached a major bridge built of iron and wood in a busy neighbourhood with restaurants and colourful shops along the riverbanks. A little further on, they got out of the car, ducked under a short grey curtain, and found themselves in a tatami room that opened onto a garden of azaleas. Paul ordered, tea and ice-cold beer were brought, as well as a lacquered box for each of them and a little wooden container with a curved stick. Rose opened the box and, on a bed of rice, found slices of fish coated in a pale brown sauce.

'Eel,' said Paul.

He picked up the little wooden container, scooped out some green powder and sprinkled it on his fish.

'*Sanshō*.'

She tasted the eel. The flesh fell in strips from a grey, oily skin. She was surprised at how sweet the sauce was, how tender the fish, how silky its texture, nothing tough or viscous about it, and how well it harmonised with the vinegary rice; she drank her beer, looking at Paul; she was glad of his silence. He finished his lunch, leaned back against the partition, stretched out his legs. With painful intensity, she wanted him to desire her, wanted him to willingly share with her who he was. *Paul is secretive, a complex personality*. Who said that? she wondered, then, Beth Scott.

'Sayoko doesn't like Beth Scott,' she said.

He raised an amused eyebrow.

'Beth isn't much liked in Kyōto; she has a reputation for being ruthless in business and not playing by the rules. She doesn't pay much attention to others when her own interests are at stake.'

'What sort of business?'

'She inherited property from her husband and turned it into a real-estate empire.'

'Her husband was Japanese?'

He nodded.

'She's very clever,' he said. 'Despite what people think of her, and the fact that she's a foreign woman, she's managed to make a name for herself here. That's quite a feat.'

'Do you get along well with her?'

'Very well.'

'And my father?'

She saw him flinch as she said *my father*.

'Haru liked her a great deal.'

'Why?'

'He liked wounded people.'

'She lost a child, didn't she?'

'You're drawing conclusions without many clues to go on,' he said.

Puzzled, she shook her head.

'It's not the first time I've noticed that,' he added.

There was something strangely gentle about his expression; she imagined he was thinking of someone else, that he had recently fallen in love with some unknown woman; she panicked at the thought that he was about to disappear from her days, her sight, her life.

'It's time to go to the lawyer's,' he said, getting to his feet.

As he was paying at the counter by the door, she noticed that his hip was hurting. He took a step towards the door, then looked back as she was still behind him.

'That wasn't a climbing accident,' she said.

A look of exhaustion passed over his face.

'No,' he said.

She followed him outside. It had started raining again. Kanto said something to Paul that made him take out his phone and make a call in Japanese. She looked around her at the passers-by, the transparent umbrellas, the streets running with rainwater. The tenderness of the moss was with her, in conflict with the depths of her sadness. I'm Haru's daughter, she thought, just the daughter that Haru told Paul to show around Kyōto. He's known about me for twenty years, he knows who I am, my emptiness, my anger. The sudden knowledge that he had seen her in photographs with her lovers was torture to her. *And all that time, he loved someone, he was suffering because he loved someone.* The car stopped in a street in the centre, beneath a torrential downpour. Kanto came round

to open the door for her and shielded her with an umbrella up to
the entrance of a sinister grey building. Paul joined her, held the
door open, went ahead of her down a labyrinth of corridors, then
through another door. An employee at a reception desk stood up,
bowed to them, and led them into an office where an elderly man
was waiting for them, along with a young woman who bowed in
turn.

'I am your interpreter,' she said.

'Can't Paul translate?' asked Rose.

'It's the law,' said the young woman. 'I'm sorry.'

She was very pretty, with clear grey eyes and a profile worthy
of a cameo.

'That's fine,' said Rose, sorry she had been so abrupt.

Paul exchanged a few friendly words with the lawyer. The man
looked like an old frog, with a wide mouth, narrow forehead, and
a lively, inquisitive gaze; on his lips was a good-natured smile; a
strange office amphibian, she thought. Everything seemed unreal.
I have been appointed to inform you of your father's last will and
testament, translated the young woman, and Rose felt she was
drowning. She couldn't concentrate any more, caught snatches of
random words and phrases that she didn't understand, struggled
breathlessly in dark, icy waters. At one point, she met Paul's worried
gaze. He stood up and came over to put his hand on her shoulder;
the gentle pressure brought her back to the surface. The lawyer
handed her a file; she didn't know what to do with it. Paul took it
for her and remained beside her. After a moment, the interpreter
asked: Did you understand everything, do you have any questions?
Rose shook her head. The young woman continued: Now there are
documents to sign. Rose looked at Paul and murmured: I want to
leave. He said a few words to the lawyer, took her by the arm, and
led her through the corridors. Standing in the entrance porch, with
the deafening sound of the downpour all around her, she gasped
for breath. We're going home, said Paul. In the car, she began

to sob uncontrollably. He put his arm around her shoulder, said something to Kanto, who made a quick telephone call, put his lips to her temple, stroked her hair. Everything was suddenly falling apart; she sobbed even harder, like a child. Outside the house, the pain of feeling Paul move away from her was unbearable. Sayoko was waiting for them on the raised floor with a length of fabric in her hands. She wrapped it around Rose and, holding her close, led her into the maple room. On a low table were steaming bowls of tea; lightly scented incense was burning; Rose collapsed on the floor. Paul spoke in hushed tones, Sayoko nodded her head. He sat down next to her.

'Get some rest; I'll come back later,' he said.

Through her tears, she shook her head, but he walked away and, after a final exchange with Sayoko, left the house. Sayoko knelt down, wiped Rose's cheeks with a handkerchief. Abruptly, Rose got up, ran to the hall and out into the garden, barefoot. On the other side of the gate, by the car, Paul was closing his umbrella.

'Don't go,' she cried.

He let go of his umbrella, walked back towards her, and, as she stood motionless in the pouring rain, he held her close. Sayoko came out, and they led her back inside. Paul bent over her and gently smoothed her hair away from her face.

'I'll be back soon,' he said.

'Please,' she begged, and took his hand, realising after she spoke that she'd called him *tu*.

He pulled his hand away, she looked down, didn't want to watch him leave. The lawyer's words were coming back to her in bursts. She was to inherit all her father's property; he had left a letter for her, to which Paul had added the one he had read at the funeral. She lay down. An hour went by. Sayoko came to tell her that she was going out, that Paul would be there for dinner, that she must get some sleep. Rose remained silent. After a short while, her phone rang, she saw *Paul* light up the screen. She heard him say: Rose, don't worry, I'll be there tonight. Come back now, she murmured. He hung up. She begged the maple, invoked the temple mosses, their call, their light touch. She heard a noise, went to the hall, slid the front door open, and found herself facing Paul.

She laughed. He took a step forward and kissed her.

11

It is said that during the Ashikaga shogunate, Sesshū, the master of ink and wash painting, was the true inventor of abstract painting. He was a great master of drawing and composition, but he liked nothing better than to splash a blank scroll with random drops of ink. One day, a rich client, surprised by such a whim, asked him what he expected to produce from it. The branch of a cherry tree, answered the artist, and before the astonished nobleman's eyes, he transformed black fireflies into a branch smothered in petals. Painting is just improvisation, then? asked the nobleman. The world is like a cherry tree one has not looked at for three days, answered Sesshū.

The World Is Like a Cherry Tree

He held her close to him as far as the room, looked in her eyes while they undressed; she felt as if she were seeing a man's body for the first time. When he entered her, she held him tightly, desperately eager; he put his arms round her back, and held her with equal force, burying his face in her neck. The sensual enjoyment was masked by an unfamiliar, more powerful sensation – this is *intimacy*, she thought suddenly, and the intoxication of this discovery mingled with her pleasure. Later, he looked again into her eyes, and she felt tears running down her cheeks. He came with a cry of relief, of wrenching sorrow, of gratitude. The intensity of their intimacy overwhelmed her; other men had never fully inhabited their bodies for her; it thrilled her to think that this body was Paul's. He lay on his back and wrapped his arms around her, but, after a moment, he pushed her gently away from him and gazed at her. They fell asleep to the sound of the rain. Before long, Rose awoke with a start. She was alone. She sat up, heard water running, fell back against the sheets. Paul came out of the bathroom, dressed, his hair wet. He crouched down next to her.

'Sayoko will be back soon,' he said. 'I'll take you out to dinner.'

She studied his eyes; he pulled her up, held her close to him, and kissed her. She had a shower and got dressed, put on lipstick, went into the maple room.

'Sayoko will be here soon,' he said.

In the hall, she paused by a tall black earthenware vase, erupting with branches of frothy white lilacs.

'Rose,' he called.

They fled through the sodden garden. In the car, he put his hand on hers, gave brief instructions to Kanto, made a phone call. The end of the day was deepening into a twilit brilliance; a harsh, tapering light seeped from the dark sky, fringing the clouds; the streets sped by like comets. Again the centre, a dark passageway, a lift to the top floor. They didn't speak, looked at each other. At the top, they came out into a room one side of which was made entirely of glass, apparently frameless; the join with the walls was invisible. The mountains of the East slept there like mute giants, as light poured down from unseen sources. To the right, in an alcove, a clay vase was bursting with unfamiliar branches. They were led to a table by the picture window, and the sake arrived at once. Paul poured and leaned back in his chair. Rose waited, breathlessly.

'I'm sorry I ran away,' he began.

She tried to speak, but he stopped her, raising his hand.

'I want to tell you what this week has been like for me.'

He was smiling, she smiled back.

'I've known you for twenty years, but when you arrived, in spite of everything I knew about you, I was stunned. The photos only reveal your indifference, your sadness. I was prepared to confront Haru's daughter, and, instead, there was an unknown woman in front of me.'

He took a sip of sake.

'I wasn't expecting anyone like you.'

'And what am I like?' she asked, thinking: I ask this question every day.

'I'm still wondering.'

Then, thoughtfully: 'A forceful flower, though, for sure.'

After a moment, he added: 'Although I have to admit that you do cry at the drop of a hat.'

Sashimi was brought, he thanked the waitress, said a few words. She bowed respectfully, and Rose understood that he had asked for them not to be disturbed.

'When I saw you kneel and touch the ground in the cemetery, at that moment I loved you intensely. So I ran away to Tōkyō. When Sayoko passed on your message, I took the first train back, but didn't know what to do. I was petrified.'

Through the huge window, Rose could see the glow of the mountains, the kindliness of these motionless heroines. She felt as if she were becoming rooted in some unfamiliar substance and was afraid of being swept away, again, by the storm.

'How did Sayoko manage to pass on my message if you were in Tōkyō?'

'She took a picture with her phone.'

'She read it?'

'She doesn't speak French.'

'You don't have to, to understand.'

He looked at her, amused.

'Is peace of mind possible for people like us?' she asked. And as he did not reply, she added, 'For people who have suffered as much as we have?'

He said nothing.

'Up to now, I've never been able to find it,' she said.

'We've just spent a few days in no-man's land. Now real life is beginning. Who can tell what will happen? But I'm ready to try.'

He stroked her hand.

'I'm keen to try,' he said.

She leaned towards him; a tear rolled down her cheek.

'I can't imagine leaving this place,' she murmured.

In his gaze she saw, fleetingly, the same strange tenderness that, earlier, had made her believe there was another woman.

'Only Anna, from time to time, can make me forget the sadness,' he said. 'Tonight, it's not there. I thought it was all about survival, but maybe it's about dying and being reborn.'

She thought of Keisuke Shibata, what was left of him, his emaciated soul.

She ate a piece of tuna sashimi, and the tender, oily flesh calmed her.

'I can't go back to Haru's with you,' Paul said. 'Sayoko will be spending the night there, and Anna is waiting for me. Tomorrow morning, I'm taking her to a play. I'll come and get you afterwards.'

Disappointed, disorientated, she put down her chopsticks.

'You have two letters to read,' he added.

A woman came up to them, and Rose saw it was Beth Scott.

'Beth,' said Paul, standing up and giving her a kiss on the cheek. 'What brings you here?'

'A business dinner,' she said, pointing to a group of Japanese men at a table near the entrance.

And to Rose: 'Would you like to have tea with me tomorrow morning?'

Rose, taken by surprise, agreed. The Englishwoman said something in Japanese to Paul, and he nodded. She was about to leave, then turned and added a few words. He looked astonished, gave a short answer. Rose followed her with her eyes as she went back to her table, made the men in suits laugh, and called the waitress, who came running and bowed deeply.

'What did she say?' asked Rose.

'She told me where you'll be meeting tomorrow.'

'And after that?'

He hesitated.

'*Yononaka wa mikka minu ma no sakura kana.* The world is like a cherry tree one has not looked at in three days. An old proverb.'

She was thoughtful for a moment.

'What did you reply?'

He was silent.

'After ashes, roses,' he said, finally.

He stood up, and she followed him to the door. He waved to

Beth. In the lift, he pulled her to him and kissed her. Outside, they were caught in the rain and wind; he got into the car for a moment but left the door open.

'Who translated the letters?' she asked. 'Was it you? Will I survive? Or will Sayoko have to wrap me up in a giant shawl?'

He smiled.

'I translated the letters,' he said.

He leaned towards her, kissed her lightly on the lips, and left.

Back at the house, she went up to her room, got undressed, lay down in the dark, and was awake for a long time, until a night-time parting of the clouds revealed a silvered moon. She fell asleep with a sensation of grace. In the morning, she awoke with a start, got dressed quickly, went to the maple room, and found Sayoko at her low table.

'You meet Scott-san at eleven,' she told her. 'Kanto-san coming at ten forty-five.'

Rose's phone rang. Paul's voice said: Rose. She laughed, responded: Paul. He laughed in turn. I'll see you this afternoon, he said. She hung up. She went back to her room, took her father's letters from the lawyer's file, returned to the main room, put them down on the floor by the glass cage. Sayoko peered at her over her glasses; Rose asked for a coffee and stretched out on the low sofa. At a quarter to eleven, she left the house. A pale sun broke through a pale mist, the morning fading into grey indifference. After a short car journey, Rose got out at a modern, pale wooden building; at the large picture windows, there were sliding panels of the same light wood, their openwork like modern lace. A canal of black stone ran all around. Inside, a half-vaulted ceiling arched with slats of curved wood. Everything was about transparency, spare and uncluttered, the motionless waters reflecting the splendour of the sky. On the other side, on a green lawn, was a garden with a maple, a cherry tree, dwarf bamboo, and an orange *torii* – I could live here, she thought. She spotted Beth at the back of the room.

The decor was black and beige, sober. At the front, there were low bookshelves, and art books displayed on lecterns. Rose glimpsed images in the open books of wooden galleries, tea plantations, kimonos. Beth looked up.

'You're looking terrific,' she said.

Rose sat down opposite her. The Englishwoman's phone rang. She listened, said a few words in Japanese, then hung up, saying, 'Sayoko is watching over you.'

'What was her relationship with my father?' asked Rose.

'Her relationship? She was his housekeeper for over forty years. He would have entrusted her with his life, in addition to his bookkeeping and his laundry.'

'Does she have a husband? Children?'

'And grandchildren, like the majority of women like her, overwhelmed by duty, sacrifice, chores, and silence. Haru's death was a tragedy for Sayoko, but you'll never hear a word of self-pity from her.'

'She doesn't like you very much,' said Rose.

'That's a euphemism,' said Beth, 'but, in a way, I understand. Japanese women are a light in a prison, and here I am, a free woman, trailing my melancholy through their temples and gardens.'

Rose was brought a bowl of matcha set in the centre of a black lacquered tray. On the white ceramic, the branch of a flowering cherry ran out a few millimetres from the upper edge.

'That's unusual for the time of year,' said Beth. Her bowl was brown, furrowed, unadorned.

'Well then,' she said, 'you and Paul.'

Rose said nothing.

'Life is full of wonder,' said Beth. 'I'd misjudged you; you're not incapable of changing.'

'I can surprise you even more,' said Rose. 'Who's to say I won't throw myself in the river tomorrow.'

Beth gave a short laugh.

'There aren't many men I respect as much as I respect Paul,' she said. 'Do you deserve him? Clara was charming, she enchanted him, gave him a life that was light and luminous. You are rough, austere, absolute, you haven't charmed him, you've touched his heart. He was probably assuming that some day he'd have a peaceful life with another Clara, find that kind of happiness again, and suddenly you show up with your melancholy, your rage, and your bad temper.'

She took a sip of tea and added: 'It won't be easy.'

Rose ran her fingertips briefly around the rim of her bowl.

'You lost a son, didn't you?' she asked.

She could tell that Beth was speechless, she saw her blink, and admired her self-control.

'You've got good intuition,' Beth said, finally.

'You're hard and cold, but you look on Paul as a son,' said Rose.

Beth's smile was joyless.

'And you're hard, too,' she said, 'but you're doing me good, because I can see that you find the same relief in this place as I do.'

Rose was disconcerted.

'Anywhere else, I would find such beauty aggressive. Only here does loss seem less cruel. Why? I'm not sure I really want to know, I'm afraid this respite might vanish into thin air. But when I walk through these gardens that are as sharp as stone, as soft as moss, I become a different woman, someone who, for a brief moment, can accept what happened. You don't survive the death of a son; you're transformed into someone else who, from time to time, finds a way to breathe again.'

She looked at Rose, her gaze sad and tired.

'I've liked you since we first met,' she said, 'and believe me, that doesn't happen often. You're about to stake everything, win or lose; don't ruin your chances.'

'That's an interesting question,' said Rose. 'Can you lose what you haven't yet received?'

As she was saying *received*, she thought of Paul with such intense desire that she had to lower her eyes.

'The hardest thing is not being able to give any more,' Beth replied. 'I was once a woman who loved, who would have walked through fire for the person I loved. I lost that, through my own fault, and since that day I've been more dead than alive.'

She gave a laugh, full of weary irony, and elegantly swept her hand over her forehead. She pointed to Rose's bowl.

'The flower of the cherry tree has great power. Its prettiness is a mask. With its spirit, its exuberance, it is all ruthless appetite and lust for life, the urge to try or die trying.'

'But in the end it does die,' said Rose.

'In the end we all die, yes,' said Beth, 'so we might as well let life improvise the music we play.'

She squeezed Rose's hand affectionately.

'Otherwise,' she said, 'it's hell before hell.'

She pulled her hand away and stood up.

'His name was William. He was twenty when he committed suicide. It was thirty years ago, it was yesterday.'

Rose watched her walk away, upright and distinguished in her unfathomable pain. Then she left the tea house, too, and asked Kanto to take her home.

In the deserted maple room, she went over to the letters lying on the floor, saw again the branch of the cherry tree dying just there by her lips, imagined the flowers, the exuberance of their petals – their appetite, voraciousness, their mad urge to try and to live. She broke the seal on an envelope, read the first words, and put the sheet of paper back down on the table. Rose, her father wrote, the world is like a cherry tree one has not looked at for three days.

In the chaotic times of the Japanese Middle Ages, which chroniclers of the era referred to as *an upside-down world*, there was a samurai and aesthete, equally skilled in the arts of the sabre and of calligraphy, who periodically returned to his home in Kagoshima on the island of Kyushu. There he was reunited with his wife and son and, in the inner garden surrounded by wooden galleries, a magnificent maple tree. When the boy was old enough to express his desire to explore the archipelago, his father pointed to the tree with its flaming autumn leaves and said: Every mutation can be found within it, it is freer than I am; be like the maple and travel inside yourself.

Be Like the Maple

S he took the other letter and opened it. Paul had handwritten a short introduction: *I won't translate the opening formalities with the names, titles, and polite phrases; I'll begin with the statement itself.* She was moved by his broad, regular handwriting. Underneath, the text had been typed, then printed on thin paper. At the end, Haru had signed with his seal. He wrote: *At the gates of death, I find myself confronted with the urgent need to tell you what I have kept from you for nearly my entire adult life. Forty years ago I fell in love with a Frenchwoman. From this ephemeral love, a daughter was born, who will soon come to Kyōto to hear my last will and testament. She did not know me, but she will know you. As your servant, who is for ever indebted to you, I humbly ask you to provide her with a warm welcome.* Rose's hand was trembling. Again she saw the cemetery, its quivering wooden strips, its lichen-covered stones, its stairways for ghosts; she imagined Paul at Haru's grave, a few steps from his wife's grave, a few steps from Nobu's; she pictured him, before that, reading this letter to a silent gathering. She put the sheet of paper down on the table and picked up the first letter again.

Rose, the world is like a cherry tree one has not looked at for three days. Yesterday, you were a joyful child, a wounded adolescent, an angry young woman, but the world turns so quickly that I am writing to a woman from the past when it is to the woman you are becoming that

I would like to write. In the hour of one's death, it is remarkably easy to draw up the inventory of one's life. Everything has been sorted; all that remains are the bare bones of existence, reduced to the marrow. Nothing, I know now, has been more powerful than your arrival in the world. Of the forty years that have since gone by, what matters most is that I have loved you. What sort of father would I have been if, after decades of absence, I had inflicted the burden of my illness upon you? What could I have given you that I cannot give you through my words? They spare you the sight of this wretched body, the terror of lost battles, love turned to punishment. Instead, I must share my fatherly pride and my joy that you have been part of my life. I have watched you grow, fall down, get back up, still whole, still unique, still unhappy. Here in Japan, our tormented islands have taught us the implacable nature of misfortune. It is through this innate sense of doom that we have learned how to transform our land of disasters into a paradise; that is why the gardens of our temples are the soul of this country of catastrophe and sacrifice. Through our shared blood, you have come to know the beauty and tragedy of the world in a way that the French, nourished by their more clement lands, cannot understand. In this upside-down era that is sold to us as modern, it's your Japanese soul that has the power to transform disenchantment and hell into a meadow of flowers. Don't be angry with me for having dragged you from one temple to the next; it is a whim of mine and also a true source of hope, because I know how these places can calm and transform. Aimless walking and words, more than property and works of art, are my true legacy. You are a forceful, unpredictable, opinionated flower; I have faith in your strength and your determination, and I remain hopeful, too, that these decades of silence will not have been in vain, that through this letter, despite my death, you will accept my heart, you will receive my love. And then, without trouble or tragedy, my entire life will pass to you.

Rose lay on the floor, her arms outstretched. The maple quivered gently. I'm at home, she thought, and she laughed. Long afterwards, she heard the front door slide open and Paul's steps approaching.

He sat down next to her and propped himself on one arm as he put the other around her waist. She realised she was weeping, silently, tears as fluid and regular as rain. He stroked her forehead, collected a teardrop on his finger. She looked at him, he took her in his arms, and they went into the bedroom. She pulled him towards her, as if to save herself from drowning, and held him close as she had the day before. Will a day come, she wondered, when I will desire him differently? In the seriousness of the moment every gesture had meaning; to Rose their nakedness seemed like a miracle; the pleasure was violent, happy; Paul gazed at her like a man who has been relieved of a burden, with new joy. At the point of orgasm, his face was one she had never seen, free of sorrow, luminous. She pressed herself against him, her back to his chest, he put his arms around her, placed his forehead on the nape of her neck. Later, they looked at each other. Paul felt around behind him for his jacket and took out an envelope that bore Haru's seal.

'The original,' he said.

Kneeling, she examined the two characters in the red ink of the seal.

'It's one of the most complex ideograms in Japanese,' he added.

'It's not his name?' she asked, but at that very moment, she understood and murmured, 'Rose.'

'No one knew until he died.'

She opened the envelope and took out two near-translucent sheets of paper. The lines with their black ink looked to her like wild grasses. On the top left-hand side, above the text, a few isolated characters had gone astray, and she touched them lightly with her fingertip.

'*Beyond, the dew alone reigns,*' Paul translated.

Then, as she raised a questioning eyebrow: 'It's the line by Keisuke that Haru had carved on his tombstone.'

Again she saw the drops of rain on the moss at Saihō-ji and thought she could make out the distorted reflection of a face.

'He grew up near a mountain torrent,' she said. 'I would have imagined, instead, a poem about icy water.'

'Haru saw life as a river to be crossed, with waters so deep they have become black. One day, I heard Keisuke say to him, You've got it right, the dew is on the far shore.'

She sensed an unfamiliar whispering within her and looked again at the text of moving grasses.

'It's beautiful writing,' she said.

'Haru was a merchant, a samurai, but above all an aesthete.'

'A true Japanese,' she remarked.

'Not for everything,' he said. 'In some respects, he was atypical, he didn't share the tastes of Japanese men of his generation. He had no intention of getting married or starting a family; he didn't spend time with geishas, let alone hostesses. There were quite a few Western women in his life.'

'Was Beth one of them?'

'Yes.'

'She loved Japanese men?'

'She loved all men. She had many lovers, even when she was married.'

'I've had a lot of lovers, too,' said Rose.

'So I saw,' he said with a smile. 'But you weren't married.'

'I don't remember any of them,' she murmured.

He fell silent.

'Why didn't Haru leave you anything?' she asked.

'I refused.'

He sat up, grimaced.

'We'll talk about it later,' he said. 'Sayoko will be coming, and I want to take you somewhere.'

'Why do you limp?' she asked.

He didn't answer, went to the bathroom, and came out showered and dressed. She was struck by how relaxed his features seemed, by the light in his eyes; she got up and went over to him; he held her in his arms, kissed her, laughed with the light-heartedness of a child. She had her shower and got dressed in turn, and went to

137

join him in the maple room, seized with a sudden reverence. The tree rose up towards ashen clouds, its branches spread like wings, its leaves trembling, reaching out to the great invisible blaze. What's happening? she wondered. She looked at the sky with its grey clouds, heavy with turbulence and storm, and the maple grew even taller.

'Rose?' Paul called, from the hallway.

She tore herself away from her contemplation of the tree in flight, began to walk away, then turned back one last time and, on impulse, bowed. In the hall, Paul held an umbrella out to her, but just as she was walking towards him, she saw the frothy profusion of white lilac, stopped again, tried to catch a fleeting thought. She went closer to the dishevelled clusters on the tender mass of foliage and felt the thought fade. She followed Paul; in the car, she took his hand and lifted it to her lips. They were speeding eastwards. Kanto stopped by a wide avenue of pine trees and azalea shrubs that went up the hill. The avenue led to a tall carved wooden gate with a thatched roof, then continued to climb beyond it. It was drizzling, they walked slowly.

'Two years after Clara's death, Keisuke and I jumped into the river,' he said. 'We were completely drunk. We climbed over the railing of the Sanjo bridge, I landed on a rock, he landed without injuring himself. Afterwards, at the hospital, he said: Hell is when even death doesn't want you. But hell, to me, was that I had failed Anna.'

'What did you tell her?'

'The truth. That her father was an idiot who had drunk too much.'

He laughed.

'She was four years old. She said, Then drink just a little.'

The avenue narrowed; finally, it reached a stone wall; through a metal gate, they could see tiers of tombs.

'Translating Haru's letter was difficult,' he said. 'His decision, years ago, was difficult. I wish you had known him.'

He stopped at the metal gate.

'Where are we?' she asked.

'Higashi Ōtani.'

'Who is here?'

'No one I know. But it's an important gathering place for the celebration of Obon, the feast of the dead.'

They entered the cemetery which perched on the hillside, with dozens of rows of closely aligned graves, a mad tide of mute grey stone. The cries of crows broke the silence; she liked their strange, croaking call. Paul took the path towards the upper levels, she followed him along stairways that changed direction, arriving, breathless, behind him at the top row. He was leaning against a railing; she joined him, took in the view. At their feet, the gigantic mausoleum; beyond, the panorama of the sky, and Kyōto, the city of wonders; in the distance, the dark summits of Arashiyama unfolding against the twilight. It had stopped raining, the sky was ghostly, ashen, edged with black streaks that fringed the clouds.

'Tell me about Obon,' she said.

'During Obon, the spirits of ancestors are honoured; they are thanked for their sacrifices, people visit their family tombs, sometimes far from home, offerings are made to the dead to relieve their troubles. The festivities last a month, but for the grand finale ten thousand lanterns are lit, here, at Higashi Ōtani.'

'Offerings to relieve the dead of what troubles?'

'It is said that *Obon* derived from a sutra in Sanskrit that means "hanging upside down in hell".'

In this upside-down era, she thought, then: Everything has been upside down in my life – I know my father through the child he once was and through the man I desire. Paul was looking at her, she drew closer to him, he put his arm around her. Below them, Kyōto was disappearing into the night. All around, the graves, damp with dew from a far shore, quivered with the invisible life of the dead. Paul kissed her on the temple.

'We're survivors,' he said, 'until others survive us.'

And so, there in the great necropolis of souls hanging upside down, Rose became someone else. In a flash, she saw the maple again, in its glass cage: rooted in the fluidity of the moss yet open to the sky, spreading life all around it in its endless variety, it whispered music to her, a music of foliage and breezes; she let herself drift on it without fear, without anger; at the edges of her perception her father's gardens and a few branches of white lilac glided, a farandole in which trees and flowers merged. She breathed in, smelled the fragrance of earth and stone, of the end of things. She realised that Paul was weeping, without sadness, surrendering to his tears, to her presence, to his desire for her. She let out a silent cry, a terrible, magnificent cry, which brought her birth and death – and rebirth, at last.

'There is only love,' said Paul. 'Love and then death.'

Acknowledgements

Thanks and gratitude to Jean-Marie
Laclavetine, Pierre Gestède, Jean-Baptiste
Del Amo, Elena Ramírez Rico.